GREGORY EL HARVEY

THE

AUTONOMOUS

ASSASSINS

I0601873

A NOVEL

Books by Gregory El Harvey

JACKSONVILLE

Autobiographical
FACES IN THE SHADOWS

Serial
THE PATTERN OF A SNOWFLAKE
DRAGONS MORE DECENT THAN MEN
DRAGONS IN LOVE
TO DIE IN THE COLDEST WINTER
THE AUTONOMOUS ASSASSINS

Cover painting: *Two Arenas* by Gregory El Harvey
(www.gregharveygallery.com)

To those who live authentically.

ACKNOWLEDGMENTS

I am grateful to Myanna Harvey for critically reading the manuscript and to Cassia Harvey for helping with the publication process.

CHAPTER 1

Lancaster County, Pennsylvania, August 2016

Catching a streak of pearl white through the curtain of the front door, Margaret Swift-Jones Packard quickened her steps. When she opened the door the Bentley had completed its horseshoe turn around the fountain and come to a stop before the front steps of the Big House. She did not rush to help with the luggage, but simply stood to watch. Ever since childhood she had loved elegance.

"Hi, Mary, welcome back," she said as the passenger-side window was lowered. She could not help but take in the brown hair, the expensive summer clothes. "Need help?"

With a flashy smile, "Thank you, Maggie, it is good to be back, indeed. No need for help though, thank you. Is Bradley around?"

She returned the smile not only out of genuine affection but also because, of all the people she knew, only the aristocratic Mary Coldgrave would use the word *indeed* like that. "Yes, of course," she replied, catching sight of Bradley coming from the old stables where the team's vehicles were parked, "he's coming now. You look a little tired, Mary."

With a chuckle, "Exhausted."

"You've traveled some miles, I think you might need a drink."

"Of course. Oh, and some of your tea, Maggie. You said you'd have the tea on."

But as Coldgrave swung open her door Bradley Hopkins caught it and said, "Hey, Mary, how about I bring your stuff in and park the machine?"

"That would be lovely, Bradley," she replied, swinging her legs out.

He could not help grinning. Somehow just being near money always made him grin. He also chuckled to himself as he noted the shooting gloves. "I'll try not to scratch it. Bentley Continental, half a million bucks—I'll handle it with gloves, just like you do."

She turned, gave him an affectionate look, and said, "Don't worry about the car, it's just paint."

Oddly, he was embarrassed by the look, so he turned from her quickly to get the luggage. Grabbing the fine leather bags, he recalled how, not three years before, on the Black Moshannon project, he had said to her quite menacingly in the restaurant that she would look less conspicuous if she would simply take her shooting gloves off, and then how the next summer, during the Atlanta project, she had saved his life. After Atlanta he was freed from despising her. Taking up the last bag, he smiled to himself that she would tell him not to worry about the car, that it was just paint, for of all the people he knew only she, stinking rich and having grown up among New York's posh elite, would say something like that. He stepped back and looked at the car. Although anomalous here in Amish country, it would go very well in Monte Carlo. No, she had no concept of money or of the cost of things, that if he really were to scratch that exquisite paint it would cost many thousands to refinish. He was glad he no longer felt compelled to despise her, but was free to accept her for who she was.

Removing the gloves and tossing them onto the bed, Coldgrave looked up at the photograph—the girl, the dog, the pool, so idyllic. She was very tired, even sleepy. If she were just to slip under the covers, she could probably sleep until the next morning. Why had Bob asked her to his picnic, his silly rustic event? She pictured him across the table from her there in the bar as he worked himself up to asking her, his expression as he then formed the words. But life was like that, a farce with a cast of dysfunctional characters. And she of course was one of them.

She turned as Bradley pushed the door open and strode in carrying her luggage, a big grin on his face. He was another one, this ex-Air Force man, this ex-middle school principal. He might appear to be every one of his forty-nine years, but when he spoke about nearly anything, especially about his .45 or his Corvette, as he so liked to do, he communicated that really he had never quite made it out of his teens.

"Where do you want these?" he queried, tossing them onto the bed without waiting for a reply. "How about here?"

"Surely, Bradley," she returned, "that's fine, thanks so much."

"Just helping out." He had not been in her room often. He eyed the bottles of liquor on the dresser. "And you're in the garage with no scratches, how about that?"

"Excellent, thank you. I am so tired. Tell Maggie, would you, that I'll be down in a minute."

"Will do. See you then."

Closing the door after him, she wondered how Gretchin, twelve years his senior and savvy as you could get, had ever brought herself to marry such a pragmatic man. She could see them still as they stood there by the pool earlier that summer saying their *I do's* and looking into each other's eyes. But at least Gretchin now had her man, something other than her dragon tattoo to climb into bed with each night and wake up with each morning.

At the dresser, she pulled the diamonds from her ears, moved the bottles of gin and whiskey, and dropped the glittering pieces into the top drawer of the case. After checking herself in the mirror, she retouched the lower lip with deep red, then looked into the brown eyes. Yes, she was one of them, one of the strange animals in this menagerie.

When her phone chimed she took it from her purse, checked its screen, and opened it. "Hi, Bob. . . . Yes, I did thank you, a little while ago. . . . No, that's fine, no need to apologize, I just didn't want to go, that's all. . . . No, no harm done. . . . I didn't consider it to be romantic, so don't worry about it.

. . . Surely, I understand. I don't see any conflict at all. . . . I am tired, yes, but I'm looking forward to some of Maggie's dark tea. . . . I'll tell her that, thanks. . . . Surely, Bob, okay. . . . Bye." Then she returned the phone to the purse and went into the bathroom.

She was late for dinner, but pulled her chair up to the table as the others were talking. It was good to hear the ambient sound of their voices. She could not say that she loved the team, but certainly she had grown closer to them. Before, as their contact and hence more their boss, she could view them quite objectively. But after she had been replaced by Bob Willard and sent to live and work with them as team leader, her view became quite subjective. Upon moving in she had seen them merely as colleagues, but after going through the heat of battle with them on the projects, she had come to see them more as family. Looking around at them now as they chatted, she felt herself relax for the first time since coming home.

"Mary," said Maggie, coming from the kitchen with a steaming bowl of corn, "how was Marseilles?"

"Oh, quite beautiful, as always. I have a few friends there, and we had drinks and watched the boats on the sea. Yes, quite beautiful, thank you."

Maggie's husband, the notorious Leonard Packard, cleared his throat and mumbled crustily, "It would be too expensive, I think."

Handing the bowl to Gretchin to begin the pass around the table, Maggie merely smiled and took her seat beside him. "I didn't say I wanted to go, Lenny," she saide, "so don't get your blood up."

"Mary, any word from Willard?" queried Gretchin soberly, scooping out a modest helping of the corn. "New project maybe? I'm sure he'll be after us soon."

"I saw him in New York," was the reply. "He took me for drinks and then asked me to go with him to his church's Halloween picnic."

Bradley cocked his head. "That would be Labor Day, Mary, I think. People have parties at Halloween, not picnics."

After taking some of the corn, then passing the bowl, Coldgrave replied, "Oh, yes, surely. Thank you, Bradley. Yes, it was for Labor Day, of course it was."

Reaching for her tea, Maggie looked at her for this, but not critically, for she, as the rest, had come to like the woman. Her eyebrows raised, Maggie now queried, "So, do you think Bob's invitation was romantic, Mary?"

With a sigh. "I think so."

"And did you accept?"

"No."

Gretchin smiled. "Why not?"

Another, but softer, sigh. "I'm afraid I told him that I simply wasn't interested—either in him or in going to his rustic event."

Bobbie Lee, exchanging a look with Connors, worked hard to suppress a chuckle at this. Neither of them cared for Willard, who had once brought his religion with him after being invited to stay the weekend, and who had asked them one by one as to their own religious leanings.

"You were gentler than that, I hope," said Gretchin.

Coldgrave lifted her water glass to her lips, but without taking a drink, put it back down. "No, I'm afraid I wasn't."

Watching this, Maggie pushed her chair back. "Mary, can I get you a drink? Sapphire on ice?"

Giving a nod and following Maggie with her eyes as she left to get the gin, she continued, "I wasn't harsh, but no, I wasn't gentle either. I just was matter of fact. I simply don't care for him."

"I'm not sure any of us does," returned Gretchin. "Professionally, of course, I mean. We didn't like Paul either. Paul Kessler—what an asshole. The guy gave me the creeps every time he opened his mouth. And sleeping with him? Jesus, I can't imagine being that guy's wife. And Willard's just about as bad. So, good for you, Mary. Wait for a better choice."

When the drink arrived, Coldgrave took it, drank half of it, then set it next to her plate, as if to say that obviously the drink was her real dinner and the food a mere side dish. They all took a moment to watch her do this. They had witnessed it countless times before, since her drinking seemed nearly perpetual. But the sheer theater of her putting alcohol to her sensual ruby lips and drinking it down like water, somehow never failed to fascinate.

CHAPTER 2

New York City

Bob Willard looked at the stack of files. Since taking over as contact for the team he had perused the contents of each folder seemingly countless times and now simply knew every detail by heart. Which was good, since he had been summoned by the new section leader to give a summary of the team's progress. But although confident he could do this effectively, still he felt his sweat begin to break out as the man now spoke.

"Tell me what they're like, Bob, this team of yours. They sound like a bunch of nuts to me. I'm sure they're not, but tell me more about them, what they're like."

Instead of answering immediately, he simply stared, which was not good, then said timorously, feeling himself swallow, "Yes, sir, sure. They're certainly a colorful crew, sir. I like them a lot."

"*Colorful* crew, cute. But I'm not one for alliteration, Willard, and I'm kind of in a hurry, so skip that kind of thing." And after pausing to give an exaggerated sigh, "Well, we're all being moved around, and since I'm new to this section, I'm trying to get crash-coursed, if you will, on the teams. So, please fill me in on yours."

Straightening himself up before the obviously impatient man, "Yes, sir. First there's Mary Coldgrave. She's quite a character, sir. She has an unbelievable knowledge of guns, just unbelievable. She's an agency-recognized small arms expert, if you know what I mean."

"I don't want to know what you mean, Bob, just tell me, okay?"

Swallowing hard, "Yes, sir, sure, okay. Mary Coldgrave, now the team leader, formerly the contact. I took over as contact when she was semi-demoted following a project in Florida, during which the then team leader Martina Osipov was killed. Mary—I mean, Coldgrave, sir—appointed Martina's husband, a former Russian infiltrator, to temporarily lead the team to finish the project."

"I kind of got that from the files, yes. He was spying here for the Russians. The bastard."

"I believe he was a societal infiltrator, sir, which is different."

"That's like saying a trash collector is a sanitation technician. No, Willard, it is not different, the man was a spy."

Avoiding the disapproving, even hawkish eyes, he cleared his throat and continued. "In any case, sir—"

"No, no, no, don't say *in any case.* Say it straight, the man was a spy. What's so difficult about that? What, are you one of these pussies who can't say a spade's a spade? The man was a damn spy, right here in our country, a bonafide Russian spy, say it."

Meekly, "Yes, sir. But he was very well liked by all the team."

"So what? A spy. . . . But go on, I'm in a hurry."

"Well, the Agency didn't like what she did. Nor did they care for the subsequent bravado and brutality shown by the team when they deliberately burned the targets' house down in the somewhat wealthy residential area. So, Coldgrave was sent to be team leader herself as a learning experience. All I can say about it, sir, is that she is quite proficient in her new role."

"Great. Go on."

Cheerily, "Well, she's thirty-nine, same age as me."

"That's irrelevant. I saw her picture—good looking."

"Yes, sir. Quite. She's, uh, uncommonly feminine."

"I'm sure she is, Bob, good for her. The marvels of glamour products, right?"

"Well, she's just naturally extremely beautiful. She has this eye that doesn't line up as she looks at you, but looks a little out to her left. It sort of enhances her beauty and gives her a sort of exotic look. It's incredible."

With a grunt to cut the description short, "And she's rich, is that right?"

"Extremely. Grew up that way, high-society New York. You should see the car she drives."

With a shake of the head, "What the hell's she doing with us, why would somebody who's rich want to be in the CIA?"

"I have not figured that one out, sir—total mystery."

"She should be out playing that game, you know, knocking wooden balls around the yard. . . . Oh yes—the file said she's a bit of a drinker?"

"Um—that is correct."

With a frown, "Is that going to be a problem?"

He hesitated. "It hasn't been yet, sir. At least, not on record. But she does—drink—sorry."

"Stop apologizing, would you, Bob? Organizations like ours attract all kinds of people, let's face it. When we need someone, we need them, that's all, and that means the whole package."

"I understand."

"And how about this Gretchin Wheeler—or I guess it's Hopkins now?"

Clearing his throat, "Yes, sir."

"Stop sirring me, okay, Bob? Just give me the gist. Is she good?"

"Sure, yeah, great. But a loose cannon, loose mouth, totally disrespectful. She's reliable and a good shot. Sixty-one years old. Her husband, Bradley Hopkins, is ex-Air Force, thoroughly patriotic, but kind of a kid with his mouth. He's forty-nine."

With a snicker, "She must be having fun with him."

"She picks on him a lot."

"Okay, Bob, quickly, give me the rest. My meeting's in ten minutes."

"Right. Kelly Connors, age forty-three. IRA. Killer, heart of blood and death. Considered extremely dangerous, even to the Agency. Bobbie Lee Henry, age thirty-eight. Confederate nationalist type. Muscles like a man, great prowess, usually rides a motorcycle, with Connors on the back. They kind of work as a team within the team. An extremely effective duo. Leonard Packard, sixty-eight, retired, runs the Estate, the place where they stay. Crusty old killer. Margaret Swift-Jones Packard, his wife, was very close to Martina Osipov, who was killed. She's seventy-two years old and quite refined in her ways. Now the team's housekeeper. And that's about it."

"They're all officially Agency though, right?"

"Sort of."

Another snicker. "Yeah, I know, so we can get rid of them fast, right? I know Kessler's theory was considered somewhat proven, but a lot of it's been luck, which is bullshit. Luck is always bullshit. Give me a regularly trained agent every time. Bunch of ad hoc nuts, no thanks. But I like results, and so far your team's delivered. Let's hope they keep it that way, or we'll lose them fast."

"I understand, sir. I kind of see it the same way."

Getting up to leave, "Good. Give them a new project."

"Yes, sir, will do."

Once back in his office Willard returned the files to the cabinet. Taking to his chair, he put his head back, looked at the ceiling and exhaled with a long sigh. The meeting might have gone so much worse. He could have been completely humiliated and made to grovel before the man. Why were section leaders always so darned proud? The tough stuff, the bully stuff, the nonsense used to build the accepted barrier. If you didn't resist their authority, still they had to make you appear to do just that.

He got up, went to the cabinet, and pulled the drawer out. After snatching up her folder, he pushed the drawer home, then sat down at the desk. Momentarily he flipped the cover open and looked at her picture. Why had he asked her to the picnic, what emotion could have induced him to do such an imprudent thing? He felt himself redden as he recalled the situation—his tricking her into coming home from her vacation, their going for drinks, his asking her to the picnic, her turning him down. And what had his attraction to her meant, that he was in love with her? Probably just a simple chemical infatuation. He looked down at the picture. She was so pretty. Closing the folder, he opened his phone, and placed the call.

"Hello, Mary, how are you, how is everyone? . . . Good, that's great. . . . Yes, right. Listen, Mary, I have a new project for the team. When would be good to visit and explain things, do you think? . . . Uh, that would be fine. I'll see you all then. . . . Sure, dinner would be great, give Maggie a definite yes for me. . . . Okay, sure. All right, I'll see you then. Bye."

CHAPTER 3

The Big House

Pulling the door open, Maggie waited before placing a perfunctory smile on her face, for Willard had not exited his sedan. When she realized he was on his phone she nearly reclosed the door, but then he got out, so she readied the smile and her usual cordial greeting.

"Come in, Bob," she said. "You're alone today. That's fine. Just go right in, they're all waiting. I'll bring you something, iced tea?"

He returned the smile, but suddenly became worried that his being alone might negatively affect his presentation to the team. "Yes, Maggie," he replied, stepping past her, "it's just me, I'm afraid, no mascot this time."

Not everyone looked up as he took his usual seat on the couch. Clearing his throat and looking around at them, he felt himself growing uncomfortably warm, perhaps from the August heat, perhaps not. There was the infamous Packard, with his grotesque magnums slung under his arms in the shoulder rig. He hadn't bothered to look up to acknowledge him, but continued to stare down at the floor like some psychotic ghoul. And Bradley, an amiable smile on his face as he gave a little wave. Beside him, Gretchin, not the simpering wife by any stretch, but more the mob boss bitch. Goodness, she looked hard! Then Connors, with her mystically beautiful face and colorless eyes. Briefly he imagined her pulling the .38 from the bra holster, but then quickly moved on to Bobbie Lee, with her muscles and gritty look. The two of them, he had always noticed, were uncommonly close. Finally, and like an oasis, Mary, with her mesmerizing beauty and aura of wealth. But if he found her smile friendly, he also instantly recognized the deliberation behind the distance it communicated.

"Hello, Bob," said Coldgrave, a twinkle in her eye. "You had a good trip, I trust. And you're alone, isn't that interesting."

Instantly Gretchin piped, her tone distinctly mocking, "The Agency's making you drive yourself, huh? I'm sure that's not because they're cheap though."

He gave her a look for this, but decided to ignore the comment and respond instead to Coldgrave. "Yes, I came alone, Mary. And it was a good trip, yes. But it's hot out there, my goodness. Midsummer's always hot, it seems."

Here Bobbie Lee sniggered out a mocking *Yep, Bob, sure is*, but Bradley, who liked Willard, offered an amiable grin and said it was hot enough to burn up a car's AC.

"Yes," replied Willard simply, attempting to return the grin. Then suddenly he brought his hands together with a pop and queried whether anyone had been swimming. But instantly feeling it had been a stupid question, he shrank back into the couch cushions. It was, he knew, useless trying to adjust to them. They were crazy, practically certified. Besides, they had obviously never liked him. And he was trying to relate to them, just why?

For a few moments they just looked at him. And Bobbie Lee, as if to say his query was not worth a polite response, took a chuggy drink from her bottle of beer and then burped.

"Well," offered Maggie, drawing up the tea cart, "we do swim a lot around here, but then, you already knew that, I'm sure, Bob. Why not stay for a swim yourself? You will be our guest for dinner, I understand, which will be very nice."

He looked up at her. "That would, um, yeah, sure, that would be great, thanks."

"And would you like a little tea before dinner?"

He nodded and selected a cookie. A protracted polite smile on his face, he waited while she poured the tea.

Coldgrave cleared her throat. "But of course, Bob has brought us a new project, which will be exciting, I'm sure. Bob?"

His hand trembled as he took the cup and saucer from Maggie. "Yes, I have a new project for you folks, I do, and I'll get right to it here." Placing the cookie upon the saucer, and then the whole thing upon a stand next to the couch, he moistened his lips and spoke. "Now—I'm sure you've all heard of the refugee problem in Syria."

"It's sort of the only thing on the news," muttered Gretchin sarcastically. "Not that I watch the goddamn news."

He could not suppress an audible sigh. "Thank you for that comment, Gretchin."

"Oh, that's right," she returned, pleased with herself, "sorry for the French, you're a Presbyterian."

Wearily he looked around at them. Why? Why him? He could have done so many other things in life. He could have chosen an occupation that didn't require dealing with profane, disrespectful people. But life was like that, it didn't give you a chance to think, it simply put you in a job and waited for you to fail.

"Mary," said Maggie, getting up, "can I refresh that for you? The same?"

Coldgrave handed her the glass. "That would be good, Maggie, thanks, I don't want to get parched. Yes, the same, that would be lovely."

Willard cleared his throat. "Now, as I was saying, the refugee problem in Syria is extensive," and shooting a glance in Gretchin's direction, "as we all know." Then noting her roll of the eyes, he continued, "Not only has human trafficking into Europe grown to a catastrophic level, but child abduction and trafficking has, as expected, followed in its wake. But that's not our problem."

"Good," piped Gretchin, "then let's all go for a swim."

Ignoring this, he put his hands together and continued. "Your targets will be two men, both very tough, who work here in this country to coordinate at least one line of the child trafficking.

They must be stopped, and as usual, I don't mean arrested."

"How tough is tough?" asked Bradley.

Willard watched as Maggie returned with the freshened drink and handed it to Coldgrave. Then he watched, as did all, as Coldgrave put the glass just under her nose, breathed in the alcohol, then put it to her lips. He had not known anyone in all his life who could drink like this woman. He knew that at the New York office, when she was the team's contact, she would leave periodically during the day to go for a drink. He had heard that she practically lived with a drink in her hand. Over the years he had known many alcoholics, two of them in his own extended family. Some of these people he had observed to be highly functioning, responsible members of society, others not so functioning. He knew that for a few, even sniffing alcohol could send them into a kind of weird spin of complete dissipation and destruction. But he had never known anyone like this woman for a sheer capacity for the stuff. And the really strange thing, he had never seen her drunk or tipsy nor heard from anyone who knew her that she ever showed the slightest sign of intoxication. Yet she drank incessantly. He had often imagined her liver to be huge, which was unlikely with a physique as trim as hers. Now he watched nearly mesmerized as she took in an ample portion of the iced gin, held it in her mouth, then swallowed it in the most feminine way. This was followed by a facial expression that said she had not tasted anything more delicious in her life.

"Uh, Bob," said Bradley, "how tough, would you say? I'm just trying to get an idea."

"What? Oh yes, well, both are ex-military and both are armed. One has a .45, the other a magnum."

"Oh, that sounds interesting," said Coldgrave.

"Hey, hey!" laughed Bradley. "Good for them, I love .45 ACP, my kind of round." But quickly he queried, "Small arms only, Bob?"

Willard unwrinkled his brow. "We think so."

Coldgrave lowered her glass. "I once shot a man with a magnum," she said casually, "a .357, ball ammo. I shot him three times, and there were three clean holes through him when they turned him over. Which was odd, since exit holes are usually larger than entrance holes. I've never killed anyone with a .45, but certainly the ballistics are different, trajectory's different, everything's different. That's a slow bullet, you know, but big enough to produce amazing ballistics at short range."

Packard asked, "Why ball ammo?"

"He was in a car," answered Coldgrave, raising the glass to her lips.

"You had to shoot through the door?"

"I thought I might have to, but in fact he stopped and got out."

"Oh," grunted Packard with a nod. "It's hard to know which load to carry, since you can get into screwy situations when you're out there. Of course," he added, giving his stubble a scratch, "if you shoot them in the face, the load doesn't matter much. I mean, it's fun, and all that, but who can take the time to shoot people in the face? My 686 is a heavy beast and swinging it on point takes time, the sheer bulk slows a guy down."

Squinting to perceive the relevance of this conversation, Willard reached for his tea. Yes, he mused, things could have taken a different turn in his life, leaving him with a completely different set of people to work with.

"Well," continued Packard, animated by the subject and now somewhat jolly, "I guess that's why Kelly doesn't swing a magnum—it just might slow her down a tad." Here he threw a respectful grin in Connors' direction.

Connors, not one to respond to praise or usually even to be aware it was being levied, merely grabbed Bobbie Lee's beer, took a swig, then handed it back.

Willard, clearly annoyed not only by the interruption of the briefing but by the nature of the conversation, said, raising his voice a notch, "Well, to get back on track here, the two targets are very serious individuals. They've killed a few people, and these are the calibers they've used. That's all we know about their weaponry. They're not timid about killing, that's for sure. They're heartless, I'm afraid."

"Oh, like us," quipped Gretchin.

He drew a breath, as if to brace himself, but when she did not continue he replied, "Well, let's just say, they're heartless for the wrong cause. If you are heartless, Gretchin, as a member of this team, and I don't think you are, it's for the right cause."

"Jesus! That is all so pathetically moralistic. I mean, think of your words—*heartless, wrong,* and *cause.* Really?"

He sighed and hung his head. "Sure, sure, Gretchin, what words would you like me to use, what would suit you?"

"Oh God! Just forget it, Bob."

"Gretchin, you've told me about a hundred times that you're not a moralist. I got it the first time, believe it or not."

"And just where," broke in Coldgrave, "are these two?"

As he looked at her, at the soft brown hair, the Vermeer skin, the perfectly painted lips, the alluring asymmetrical eyes, he found himself unable to answer. He could not help watching as she crossed her legs. Then he heard her voice.

"Bob, the targets," she urged gently, "where are they?"

"Right," he returned, forcing his gaze away from her. "Actually they are in Pittsburgh, for now at least. Which is one of the reasons the project was slated for this team—the Agency felt that since Pittsburgh wasn't too far from this team's base, well—" He broke off, a sheepish look on his face.

Maggie cocked her head. "Well what, Bob?"

Clearing his throat, "The Agency felt it wouldn't be an expensive trip, since you're fairly close to Pittsburgh."

Gretchin gave her head a shake, spreading out the grayed red hair like a flame. "Oh my God," she burst out, "an expensive trip? What are we now, discount assassins?"

"No, Gretchin," he pleaded meekly, "not at all."

She was incredulous. "They're concerned about the expense of the goddamn trip?"

"Things have been tight everywhere," he said, avoiding her fiery eyes. "You can't blame them for wanting to save money."

"Fuck them!" she shot back, "and fuck you too, asshole. I can blame them all I want. They want us to spread these guys' guts on the sidewalk for them, but then turn around and nickel-and-dime us for the fucking trip? Jesus."

"I think you're being too harsh."

"I don't."

Packard gave a grunt of disinterest at this. "What were the other reasons?" And when Willard merely looked at him, "You said proximity was one of the reasons—so, the other reasons?"

"Oh, yes, right. Actually just one other reason— your luck, the team's good luck. The Agency considers the team to be unusually lucky. And it has been lucky, or whatever you want to call it, anyone can see that."

"So," said Gretchin, "they want to use us while our luck holds."

He swallowed. "Something like that. After all, luck runs out, it always runs out."

With a certain melancholy in her tone, Maggie said softly, "It did for Martina."

CHAPTER 4

Following dinner, with the sun still up, they went out to the pool, lowered the umbrellas, and spread towels on the cushioned chairs. Packard and Bradley, grabbing beers, immediately set to gabbing about baseball. Willard did not join them, for he had been talked into going swimming. When Maggie rolled out the tea cart loaded with dessert, she called Packard a lug and said he would ruin his dessert with his beer. After Connors and Bobbie Lee got into the pool at the shallow end and began to splash each other and wrestle, Willard went over to watch them. It felt odd to be watching as two beautiful, nearly naked women threw each other around in the water. But life seemed to do that sometimes, he mused, it gave you strange things to look at, such as a bullet-scarred Kelly Connors and a muscular Bobbie Lee Henry. For a few moments he continued to watch as they cavorted in their bikinis.

He turned, walked to the deep end, sat down for a moment, then slipped into the water. For a few minutes he paddled in circles, relaxing in the warm luscious water, but when Coldgrave and Gretchin came from the house and walked toward the tables, he stopped, held onto the side, and watched them.

The sun now was just down to the tops of the trees. Connors and Bobbie Lee, tiring of their fun, began to swim laps. Packard and Bradley brought out a small TV and tuned in to the game they had been discussing. Maggie put her feet up and opened a magazine. And Coldgrave and Gretchin got into the pool and swam toward Willard.

"So here he is," said Gretchin, stopping to tread water, "all by himself. You know, don't you, that this Agency we all work for might be watching us?"

He let go and began to tread water with them. He looked at her, then at Coldgrave. "I wouldn't be surprised," he replied. Then in an attempt to turn things toward a lighter side, "They love me, they love all of us, and they don't want to lose us."

"Granted they love us," she returned, "and would be heartbroken if they lost us, but you have to admit that they not only could, but would, replace us in a heartbeat."

"I suppose," he replied, his eyes going to where the water licked at the dragon tattooed along the side of her neck. He felt uneasy being so close to her. As pretty and well formed as she was, he still felt repelled by her incessant and unabashed efforts to communicate her ill will toward him.

"In fact," she continued, "they might even be thinking as they watch us that they could probably get more out of our replacements than they've ever gotten out of us."

"Possibly," he said cautiously as he met her sparkling eyes. But when they narrowed he nearly caught his breath.

"Actually," she said, her tone going cold, "if they're on their toes and know their stuff, and have listened to all the shit you've probably told them about me, they know what I think of them, which is as much as I think of you." And splashing water in his face, she swam away. "Take it easy, prick!"

Wiping the water from his eyes, he turned to Coldgrave, until now merely a passive observer. "Gracious, does she ever change?" he said. "She's like a vicious dog. She doesn't like me at all, does she?"

"I think a vicious dog, if there is such a thing, might actually like you more than she does, Bob."

He looked at her. "What gives me the feeling you don't want me to swim too close to you?" And when she did not reply, "Why didn't you want to go with me to the picnic?"

There was no response. As the sun dropped with the ending of the day the water took on a distinctive emerald color and enhanced the colors of her hair, her eyes, her skin, her lips. He wished that he could alter the way society framed beauty, but he knew he wished in vain. He looked down through the water at her legs as they moved, then at what he could see of the rest of her. He did not actually know anyone so beautiful, so wealthy, so keen of mind, or so taken with alcohol. Wondering what she looked like without the swimsuit, he looked again into her face and said, "It's just a picnic."

"I know, Bob," she said at length, "but I don't enjoy rustic events, and like I told you when you pressed me in New York, I have no feelings for you."

"So, you think my invitation was romantic?"

"Yes."

Now it was he who did not respond. He looked at the wet hair, the face, the sumptuous lips. When he found himself staring at the out-looking left eye, he checked himself and looked at the right. How was it that the mismatched eyes only made her seem more exotic? But they did, at least to him.

"Was it not romantic, Bob?" she queried.

After a moment, "I suppose it was." Then, "Are you attracted to men, Mary?"

Briefly closing her eyes, "To some, I think."

"To women?"

"To some, I think."

"Don't you find that confusing?"

"No. I think life only becomes confusing when people make up their minds."

"Well," he said, "I'm someone who likes to have his mind made up. For me, life is confusing only when people aren't what they should be."

"You mean, *who* they should be?"

"No, *what* they should be."

"So, you find it confusing that I'm what I am, that I'm not what you think I should be."

"Yes. But I find it even more confusing that I'm attracted to you and so am not what *I* should be."

"And what should you be?"

"I suppose, a guy who isn't attracted to a woman so beautiful or so rich or who drinks so darn much."

"You're a mixed-up man?"

He wanted to tell her he could never be as mixed-up as she was, but instead, he answered with a chuckle, "Yeah, I guess I am."

"I'm sorry for that, Bob."

Then for some reason he felt ashamed, not before her, but within himself. He looked down again through the water at her body, imagining her without the suit. If she changed her mind and consented to go with him to the picnic, he would simply need to keep her from drinking there, for she probably carried a flask. But if something were to develop between them, where in God's name would such a relationship go? As he looked down through the water at her body he looked more deeply into himself. He wanted to say something more, but simply could not. Then he heard her speaking and looked up into her face again.

"Want a drink?" she asked. "I'm tired. Let's get out, what do you say? And I think Maggie brought dessert."

At the tables they toweled off and selected desserts, listening to the chatter of the others. Thoughtfully Maggie had placed a bottle of Sapphire and a small bucket of party ice on the cart. After pouring herself a hefty portion of gin on ice, Coldgrave took a seat next to Willard. She tipped the glass, swallowed twice, then looked up at the sky.

"Man, you sure drink a lot," he said softly.

She continued to gaze at the sky. "I do drink," she replied, "but only in moderation."

Nearby, Packard and Bradley were intent upon the game, while Maggie and Gretchin discussed their proposed renovations to the kitchen. Connors and Bobbie Lee were just returning from a walk with the dogs Tai Ping and Helga. Still in their bikinis, they unleashed the dogs, then got into the pool to cool off.

Turning her gaze upon the two women as they swam, Coldgrave brought the glass to her nose and inhaled its vapors. Bobbie Lee was pretty enough, she considered, with her long chestnut hair draped wet around her shoulders, her muscles undulating. But Connors, with her bullet-scarred ivory skin glistening with water beads, her wet blond hair smooth like a mane of molten gold, was truly an extraordinarily beautiful thing. So, she watched her now as the two swam and the summer evening approached and life seemed so attractive, yet so unbearable.

She looked over at Willard, who also watched the swimmers. Why did he have to ask her if she was attracted to men or to women? Why did he have to do that? Why was it that people made you choose? And why did you have to love anyone at all? There had been a few men, just as there had been some women. It had simply not worked out with any of them. She did not think about it much, for she preferred to think about whatever and whomever she found to be beautiful. Life without beauty was dirty, smelly, unpalatable, but with beauty life was clean, fresh, even delicious. For herself, she did not care whether it was men or women swimming in her glass of gin, as long as they liked the alcohol and were beautiful.

"So, Mary," he said suddenly, "what kind of man do you think you're looking for, would you say?"

"I'm not looking, Bob."

"Okay. But if you were?"

Momentarily, "Not really sure. Maybe one that likes to drink."

"That's funny! But I mean—like, successful? Smart? Good looking? Rich?"

"Oh, I don't know. I suppose, just someone who would enjoy sitting on a patio in the summertime with a simple glass of gin and ice."

Here he looked over at her, then back at the swimmers.

"Or," she continued, "maybe someone who would enjoy wandering a museum with a good scotch neat, or listening to Bruckner with a nice Riesling, or just sitting in a piano bar with a lovely dirty martini."

He looked at her again, then again back at the swimmers. "Okay, I can see you doing those things. Sure."

"And how about you, Bob? What kind of woman are you looking for?"

He took a moment, then replied, "I guess, someone who would enjoy just watching a baseball game on TV or even going to a church service sometime. You know, someone like that."

She nodded. "That makes sense, Bob. I certainly hope you find her."

"Yep. Me too."

"She might be waiting for you right now, Bob."

"Think so?" And with a chuckle, "That sounds great."

She did not respond further, but raised her glass to check the level. Then she got up, refreshed the drink, and grabbed the towel she had left to dry. Returning to her chair, she spread the towel over her legs, looked up at the sky, and took a sip from the glass.

Willard, however, had now put his eyes upon the dogs. He had never liked them, and they had never liked him. After many futile attempts to overcome this negativity, he had simply resolved to let it go, that somehow he must simply not be a dog person. Who could feel at ease around such monsters? But now he did relax, as both dogs lumbered over to their water dish by the back door, then stretched out upon the grass as if to enjoy the rest of the evening.

When it grew dark Packard and Bradley lit the torches, and Maggie and Gretchin brought out chips and lemonade. Connors and Bobbie Lee poured Jack Daniel's into their lemonade, while Packard, Bradley, and Gretchin added vodka to theirs. Coldgrave chose to leave her lemonade undiluted, but then hardly touching it simply looked to refreshing her Sapphire numerous times. Only Willard and Maggie chose to drink the lemonade straight.

Later, during the drive back to New York, with the dashboard lights glowing at him through the darkness, Willard tried to recall all of Coldgrave's words as she had spoken them throughout the day. He did not attempt to analyze the logic behind his doing this, but simply let himself go to follow his curiosity. He especially recalled her words to him in the pool as she had reiterated that she had no feelings for him. Which was just as well, he considered, putting his blinker on and switching lanes for the turnpike entrance. After all, if she had liked him and consented to go with him to the picnic and they were at some later point to marry, what in God's name would he do with her, go to posh bars and drinking parties with her? And turning onto the on-ramp now, he felt distinctly relieved.

CHAPTER 5

Pittsburgh, September

Coldgrave flexed her fingers in the shooting gloves, then touched the corner of the page and turned it. She looked up from the magazine as Connors and Bobbie Lee rounded the corner. She said nothing until they were seated across from her. There was no one else with them at the reading table.

"Well?" she queried, giving another page a turn.

The two had been scouting the library for the two targets and had located them with a positive identification based upon the photos in Willard's info packet.

Connors gave her nose a wipe. "The two fuckers, loike, are upstairs lookin' at maps."

Coldgrave looked up. "Please keep your voice down, Kelly."

"I'm joost sayin', Mary, d'you want me to go up and kell 'am?"

Bobbie Lee, who had pulled on her riding gloves, touched Connors' arm and in Tennessee twang said, "It's a nice day out, Killy, why not hit 'em on the bike? C'mon, it'll be fun."

Annoyed, Coldgrave said, "Please keep your voices down, this is a public library."

Connors blinked. "Nobody's here, for fuck's sake."

Ignoring this and looking down at the page, Coldgrave continued, "And since it is a very public place in a major city, it might not be the best place for us to do it. If we must do it here, then we will, but let's look at the second option."

Bobbie Lee, pulling a glove off and reaching for a camping magazine, grinned with excitement. "Good thinkin', Mary. I'd sure like a chase."

With a stern look, Coldgrave put a gloved finger to her lips to demand quiet. Then she closed the magazine. "Kelly, go up, and when they leave follow them out." And touching Bobbie Lee's jacket, "Come on, let's go."

Apathetically Connors pushed away from the table, handed her helmet to Bobbie Lee, and left.

Once outside Coldgrave called Gretchin, and moments later the SUV pulled to the curb just in front of the parked motorcycle. Getting in beside Bradley, she left the door open and sat looking at Bobbie Lee's chestnut hair as she stood in the sunlight holding the two helmets.

"Just wait on the motorcycle," she said, pushing on her sunglasses. "When she comes out you two take the lead, and we'll follow. Then just pick a good place and—cut them down."

From the back seat, Gretchin watched as Coldgrave followed Bobbie Lee in her mirror until she had climbed onto the bike.

"You can keep it running," Coldgrave said to Bradley, reaching into her purse for her lipstick.

He pushed the lever up, then relaxed. "So, I guess they were there, huh?"

"They were, and right on time. Intel was good. Kelly will follow them out, then we'll get them in the car somewhere. . . . Is there any of that beer in the back?"

He balled his fist up. "Oh no, I'm sorry, Mary, I forgot to grab the cooler. Sorry. Darn."

She sighed unhappily, but replied, "It's not a problem, I was just getting a little thirsty, that's all. It's not a problem."

But reaching over behind her seat, Gretchin brought up a cold lager. "I got it," she said, removing the cap and passing the bottle up to Coldgrave. "Here you go, Mary."

"Oh—you're a godsend. Thank you, Gretchin. I was just getting a little parched." Then immediately she tipped the bottle up and drank half its contents. "Um-m, yummy. It's a good thing I'm not driving, you know. They don't let you drink and drive anymore."

Clearing her throat, "I'm not sure they ever did, Mary."

"They're so concerned about drunk drivers, aren't they?"

"It's just a beer."

"Well, one can't be too careful, and one has to respect the law."

In his mirror Bradley caught the roll of Gretchin's eyes. With a chuckle, he said, "Bob wouldn't say it that way, Mary, he would say one *should* respect the law."

"Yes," she replied, bringing the bottle to her lips, "Bob is a little odd."

With a shrug. "Actually I agree with him."

"I'm sure you do, Bradley," she returned, looking toward the library entrance.

But Gretchin said, "I'll tell you what you should do, Bradley, you should divorce me and marry Bob."

He did not bother to find her in the mirror. "You're very funny, dear, just a riot."

In a cold tone, "Don't call me that, Bradley, don't call me that."

"And if I do, what will you do, call me something nasty?"

"You're goddamn right I will. And turn the air up, it's summer, dick." When Coldgrave held the empty back over the seat and queried if there was another, she took it and pulled open the cooler. "Here, Mary, but you might need a bathroom."

"Yes, perhaps I will. But we'll find something. . . . I loathe public restrooms, they're unbearable. Why is the public so dirty, I wonder?"

Pulling a book at random from the shelf behind her, Connors opened it upon the reading table. Twenty feet away sat the two men, numerous maps spread out before them. After reading a few words from the book, she looked around the room. Except for the two men, no one else was there. Which made sense, she reasoned, for after all, who the fuck would spend such a nice day in a library looking at maps?

Once they shot her a glance, then mumbled something low and chuckled. But within a few minutes they began to argue, then to roll up the maps. After they had returned the maps to their rack, one suggested they hit the drain before the ride home. In passing her table, the shorter one reached out and tapped her arm with his forefinger and gave a low whistle, but kept walking. At the corner of the room they entered the men's room.

She got up, returned the book to the shelf, walked to the corner, and stood in front of the door to the men's room. After counting off five seconds, she pulled the door open and strode in. Both men were standing at the urinals, gabbing raucously and giggling.

"Hey, boys," she said cheerily as she strode toward them, one hand gripping the bottom front of her top, "lat me show yous some of me equepmant."

Instantly they turned their heads, but said nothing, both grinning at her as they continued to urinate. The shorter one, who had tapped her arm, wrinkled his nose and emitted a quick little laugh.

Then, still striding toward them, she lifted the front of her top, reached up under with the other hand and yanked down the .38. Quickly she fired twice into the body of the first man—*Pop! Pop!*— then once into the body of the second—*Blat!* The first man groaned and slumped to the floor, his chin hitting the urinal, but the second gave out a yell, spun away from her, and fell down upon his hands and knees. Stepping over to him, she put the muzzle to the back of his head and fired—*Blop!*—dropping him face down. Turning, she reached under the urinal, put the muzzle to the temple of the first man, his cheek against the wall, his eyes glazed, and fired—*Blam!* Then she stood, reholstered, pulled the front of her top down, and walked out.

"Something's wrong," said Gretchin, spotting Connors exiting through the front doors and beginning to descend the steps, "there's Kelly. You said she was going to follow them. Oh God!"

Casually Coldgrave handed the second empty back to Gretchin. Pulling the sunglasses down, she dropped her window and watched as Connors approached. It soon became obvious that her face and top were covered with spatters of blood. As she was about to speak Coldgrave cut her off.

"Just tell us later, Kelly. We'll see you at home."

Without answering, Connors simply turned and walked back to the motorcycle.

Coldgrave followed her in the mirror until she had helmeted and climbed up behind Bobbie Lee. When she heard the Harley start, she said to Bradley, "All right, let's drive."

The Estate

When Connors came out from her shower, a towel around her head, she said, "Stell here?"

Bobbie Lee grabbed a magazine and sat back on the bed. "Yup. Just waitin' to catch you in your birthday suit so I can post a picture of you online."

"I could respond by postin' a pecture of your bloody carpse."

Watching as the blond hair was shaken out and toweled, Bobbie Lee offered, "You'd look real nice, girl, if you was to git some plastic surgery on them bullet scars."

"You keep sayin' t'at. You should come oop weth somet'ing new. Besoides, loike, who fuckin' cares?"

"Maybe I do."

"Not loikely."

Flipping a page, "Plastic surgery doesn't cost much. You'd be fit for one of them New York photoshoots. We could git you in some magazine, what say?"

"You and your glamour, bunch of shet."

Continuing to eye the snowy skin, "Well, you're still real pritty. It's a good thing you've never got your tits shot, girl."

Connors tossed the towel onto the bed and pulled a drawer open.

Dropping the magazine and flexing her muscles, her eyes following the elegant lines of Connor's body, Bobbie Lee queried, "Hey, when're we goin' to Tinnessee?"

"Stop askin' me t'at. Fuck's sake, I'm not goin'."

"Mimphis has some real nice nightclubs, you don't know what you're missin'."

"So what?"

"I sure miss the South, I can tellya that. . . . We could take the Harley and go out to bars and nightclubs, and I could hang my old flag off the tail. Come on, your hair and the Confederate flag a-blowin', that's as good as it gits, girl."

"Kaep et oop, I moight give en."

After a moment, "They're gonna ask what went wrong."

Strapping on her flash bra, then shoving the .38 home, "So what?"

"Well, you could tell me first. One of them wicks did somethin' wrong, didn't he?"

Momentarily, "He touched me arm and whestled. I was joost sattin' there, moindin' me own business, and whan they went past me, the short one reached out and touched me arm weth his fenger."

"Well, that's a goddamn animal, right there, I'd of shot 'im, too."

With a shrug, "What's the defferance?"

"None at all, girl. . . . Know somethin'? You look weird standin' there naked with that gun a-hangin' from that brassiere. You look good enough to have for dinner, I admit, but you do look weird."

When Maggie set a steaming peach pie upon the pad and reached for the pie knife, Bradley gave it a loud sniff and asked if there was any ice cream too.

Immediately Gretchin punched his leg with her fist. "She brought pie, okay? If you want more, get off your ass and help. Jesus! And you were in the Air Force?"

"Hey, lay off," he shot back, pushing himself from the table. "I'll get it, don't worry about it."

"Yeah, now you will."

As he left for the kitchen, "Take a joke, Gretchin."

When he returned with the frosty carton she said, "It's not a joke when you sit on your ass and make demands."

Shoving his spoon into the ice cream, "Stop."

"Yeah, and you'll probably eat half the pie."

When the squabble was over Coldgrave lowered her drink and looked at Connors. "Kelly," she said, "could you tell us what went wrong today?"

"Not'in'. Two carpses, semple as t'at."

"But why didn't you follow them out as planned, where we could all lend support?"

Glancing at Bobbie Lee, Connors picked up her cup and gave it a loud slurp. "One of tham," she replied, "put 'is hand on me as they were headin' for the toilat."

Coldgrave cleared her throat. "And?"

With a quick shrug, "So, I followed tham."

"You shot them in the restroom? It was a public library. Did anyone see you?"

"I don't know, loike, I dedn't notice."

"So, then you just walked out?"

With a blink, "What'd you expact me to do, fuckin' mop oop?"

No one said anything to this. Packard merely gave his nose a wipe and asked Bradley to push the ice cream over.

Then Maggie said, "I think the top's gone, Kelly, sorry. We can bleach it, but I don't think it will do any good."

"Yeah," chimed Gretchin, "and don't expect the Agency to reimburse you for it."

Connors, as if none of this had registered, merely said, "Ice cream would be good for me too, if you don't moind, loike."

As she got into bed Gretchin gave Bradley's arm a slap. "You have to stop acting like an adolescent, you embarrassed me at dinner. You'll be fifty next year, fifty years old, and I want you to start acting like it."

"Why?"

"That's a stupid thing to say. Because I want you to, that's why. You're not a kid."

"So? Maybe I like acting young." But immediately he knew he had slipped. He had learned to avoid saying anything that might draw attention to their age difference. She was still pretty and sexy, and besides, he liked older women. In fact, he liked all women, as long as they were pretty.

"Well, you're younger than Maggie and you can get off your ass sometimes and help. Don't be insensitive."

"I do help, I help a lot. I do a lot of the work around the place, even more than Len. I shovel snow, carry luggage, I do a lot."

"It was your attitude, you were insensitive."

"I don't think I was."

"You were insensitive in spades, bub." And when he was silent she said softly, "Come on, just do what I ask, just be a little more sensitive and act a little more mature."

With a sigh, "Okay."

Touching his arm, "Do you like my new nightgown?"

"Sure."

"You didn't look."

Another sigh. "Sorry, . . . yes, I like it."

She sat up, pulled it off, and said, "Want me to sit on you?"

"Okay."

CHAPTER 6

A week later, Willard and a sidekick agent sat together on the living room couch, sipping English breakfast tea and munching cookies. Occasionally both looked around at the team. The sidekick, who had been warned about the group's oddities, kept his head lowered, lest he should elicit some confrontation. When Willard nudged him and whispered that he should try to look a little more natural the agent cleared his throat and replied that he was sorry.

As if to remedy his growing discomfort, Willard turned to Coldgrave and queried, "Okay to start, Mary, do you think?"

Coldgrave lowered her glass. "Surely, Bob, surely, go ahead, please."

Raising his head as if to present himself properly, he said, "All right, everyone, maybe we can discuss the project, if that's okay."

Gretchin cocked her head, "Oh," she said, her tone mocking, "don't tell us, you want to know how much the trip cost. Well, let's see—Bradley, didn't you spend some quarters on parking?"

Bradley sat up. "Uh, no, I didn't."

"Well, how about gas, then, what did that cost?"

Willard cleared his throat. "Gretchin, thank you, but I'm not concerned about that."

"I just thought," she returned, "that since you're our contact, which is sort of a semi-boss type thing, and you're representing the Agency, and all—"

He put his cup down. "Cute, but can we move beyond the expenses issue?"

"Why? Do you realize how much toilet paper costs us here? Or how about vacuum cleaner bags—oh, I'm sorry, we've gone bagless, haven't we? Well, how about other expenses, you must want to know about them—you know, so you can report them to the cheapest fucking intelligence agency on the planet."

Throwing the sidekick a roll of his eyes, Willard again cleared his throat. "No, Gretchin, I would not like to know about all that. And I don't have a new project. I want to know why the last project was executed the way it was. Mary and I have discussed it, but I want to voice my concerns here before you all. A library, a public library, is a kind of sanctuary, if I can put it that way. But you all know that. So?"

Gretchin smirked. "Sounds like a church."

Blinking, he replied indignantly, "It is a place where people can go and read or just browse the bookshelves. It is not a place to—"

"Fucking butcher someone?"

Suppressing his anger, "Thank you for the profanity, Gretchin, but no it is not a place to kill someone. The project should not have been carried out there."

"Look, Bradley," she said, "you've got company—here's another armchair quarterback."

Willard threw up his hands. "Stop it, Gretchin, do you mind? This is quite serious. And I would remind you, I *am* the quarterback here, and you're just a player, Gretchin, one single player. And I call the plays, not you."

"You're more like the coach, don't you think? The quarterback would be Mary."

"What difference does it make? None, that's what, so just let it go, would you?" And turning to Connors, who sat slouched with a beer in her fist, "Ms. Connors, Kelly, why did it happen? Can you explain, please?"

Connors merely offered a shrug of indifference.

"You gunned them down in the bathroom, the men's room. They were found by one of the public, for goodness' sake, before the cleanup crew could get there. And the crew described it as a gross, bloody scene. So—why?"

Bobbie Lee, as if to express her own indifference, bit into a cookie, handed the rest of it to Connors, then noisily slurped at her tea.

"Why?" he repeated, bringing his hands together. "Why did you have to do it there? Why couldn't you have gotten them away from the library? I understand that was the plan, so why didn't you stick to the plan? When I asked Mary, she said I should ask you. So, I'm asking. Please explain."

Connors merely popped the rest of the cookie into her mouth and chewed.

"Well," he said after a moment, "let me ask you this. How can I understand your actions better? What can I do here to communicate my good will?"

She swallowed the cookie. "Yous can replace me top. There was shet all over et."

He hesitated. "What was on it?"

Maggie put in, "There were blood and flesh spatterings on it. I can't get the stains out, I'm afraid."

He was incredulous. "So?"

"What's so difficult?" queried Bobbie Lee. "She wants a new shirt."

His voice nearly breaking, "A new shirt, Kelly, you want a new shirt? Getting you a new shirt would help me understand why you acted the way you did?"

"Well," said Connors, "you don't need to pretand to understand me. Joost replace the fuckin' top."

Bradley, who could not help himself, burst out with a snorty guffaw.

"Do you know, Kelly," said Willard, his eyes going shut, "that there were little kids just downstairs in the children's section? Do you know that a mother was changing her baby's diaper in the women's room just down the hall from the cartography section? She even heard the shots from your gun."

"One of the reasons for that," put in Coldgrave, giving her glass a shake to slosh the gin over the ice, "is because Kelly uses such heavy P+ loads, and her 642 has a 1.875-inch barrel. So, a lot of the energy is expelled in noise. I'm surprised they didn't hear it down at the front desk."

"They did, Mary," he replied helplessly, "they did. They just didn't know what to make of it."

"Well, that makes sense, Bob. She's getting a good amount of energy at the muzzle. And I'm sure that hurt your ears, Kelly, in a tiled bathroom." And when Connors did not respond, "I like that load myself. It's cleaner than a magnum for close work, in my opinion."

Packard frowned at this. "Use a real gun, if you ask me, even for close-up. Three fifty-seven, all the way."

Lifting her eyebrows, "But, Len, think of that kind of pressure released in a bathroom with tiled walls. The additional power of a .357 at that close range wouldn't be worth the risk to your hearing. Now, my research says a few times wouldn't damage someone's hearing, but Kelly shoots a lot, and perhaps prefers killing people in bathrooms, especially if they're men. Over a considerable period of time that could cause damage."

"Awe, who cares? If your hearing goes, just retire to the beach and you won't have to listen to the mindless sound of the breakers, how's that?"

"I don't know," she returned cautiously, "I wouldn't want to give up even a decibel of Bruckner or Sibelius. The ballistics just wouldn't be worth it for me."

As the ballistics discussion continued Willard simply closed his eyes and kept them shut. When Maggie brought Coldgrave a refresher drink he threw the sidekick a look of unbelief. But finally he saw an opportunity and spoke up.

"All I'm asking, people, is that everyone make a significant effort to make the work a little cleaner."

Gretchin gave him a look. "You're interrupting, we're not even talking about that."

"But I want to talk about it," he said. "I didn't come here to discuss ballistics, for goodness' sake, Gretchin."

"Yeah, well maybe talking about something not on your agenda would do you some good."

His mouth falling open, "I don't think you should be saying that to me, Gretchin, I really don't."

"Well you've got a whole goddamn suitcase full of shit you want to say to us."

Again throwing his hands up, "Let's just get back, if we can here, okay? I'm simply making a request, okay? I'm just asking for cleaner work from the team, that's all."

"You know somethin', Bob," said Bobbie Lee, "you remind me of people who think their meat comes from the supermarket, when it really comes from the slaughterhouse. Killin' and cuttin' up a steer ain't a clean job, buckets of blood and shit. Where's your meat come from, Bob?"

Coldgrave lowered her glass. "She has a point, Bob, you must admit."

Now hopelessness filled his face, and he sank back into the couch cushions.

"So," said Gretchin, "how about the replacement of Kelly's top, will the Agency spring for that or not?"

"Uh," he stammered, "sure, sure. I'll put in for it when I get back, just text me the cost, and I'm sure it will be all right."

"And if it isn't?"

Again raising both hands, "I don't know, Gretchin, okay? I'll pay for it myself, if I have to, is that all right with you?"

"Nobody wants you to do that, Bob, you're not her employer. Just make a good try for the reimbursement, would you?"

Nearly choking, he looked at the floor. "Sure, sure."

New York State

Willard, uncommonly attired in jeans and a polo shirt, stood in the hotdog line as all around him families from the church played softball or badminton or some other game. He felt unusually alone and had engaged in none of the activities. After Coldgrave's rejection, he had decided to pass on the Labor Day picnic and instead to attend this replay. When a finger touched the middle of his back, he turned around. A woman, cute, about in her thirties or late twenties, smiled up at him.

"Did I miss you at the Labor Day picnic?" she asked.

Now he could see she was quite pretty. As she took her sunglasses off he said easily, "I couldn't make it, I'm afraid. But it's certainly a good group today, and a lot of activities."

"You haven't done any of them. I was noticing. I wasn't watching, I was just noticing."

"Sorry, yeah, I guess you're right." And with an apologetic chuckle, "No excuses, I guess I just don't feel like participating today."

"Not a sad boy, I hope."

The levity did not bother him. In fact, it seemed to help, for indeed he was a bit melancholy. He was glad for the chance to put on a smile, and he looked closer at the wavy brown hair, the pleasant brown eyes, the milky skin. Clearly she was a clean person.

"So," she said, "what are you after here?"

"I have no idea."

"I mean, here, in the line."

"Right—a hotdog actually. . . . Oh, and you?"

"The same, I guess. I was undecided, but that sounds good, so let's have one together."

"Sure," he replied, stealing a deeper look into the eyes, "that would be great."

"There is beer, I understand, which is breaking out, if you ask me, at least for a church picnic. Do you drink?"

"Not really. I will if I have to, to keep from offending someone, or whatever, but no, no, I don't really drink."

"Same here, exactly the same. Good. My name's Sandy. I know, brown hair, but yeah, Sandy."

"I'm Bob, Bob Willard."

She put her hand out, "Sandy Rogers. Nice to meet you, Bob Willard."

He moved so she could stand beside him, and when they had advanced to the counter he let her order first. But she did not order for herself alone, but for both of them.

A table by the pond was free. Squirrels scampered as they approached, but did not go very far away, as if knowing there was nothing to fear and that the picnickers would either toss them something or leave them something. On the dark water ducks paddled and quacked, as if to provide their own natural music to the scene.

"So," he said after taking a bite of hotdog, "have you been to the church before? I don't remember seeing you at the services."

"I'm afraid not. Do you like it there?"

"I do, yes. . . . But how did you hear about the picnic?"

"I know the Kluggers, they invited me."

"Oh sure."

"Aren't the ducks beautiful? Everything is so pastoral, don't you think?"

He smiled. "It is very nice here, placid, a little dreamlike, if that's not going too far."

"I was thinking that myself, dreamlike, yes. Could I ask you something? You know the Bible, right?"

Wiping his mouth with his napkin, "Well, I'm not an expert."

"I'm sorry, but you actually look like one. Don't ask me why, I can't explain it. But why are the four Gospels sort of color-coded, purple, red, white, and blue? I've heard them referred to that way, and I've always been intrigued."

He smiled again as he began to well up with joy at the depth of the conversation. This was so different from talking with Mary. When people didn't care for religious things they never enjoyed spiritual references. A reference to the color associations of the gospels would have flown right past Mary. He looked across at the brown eyes, the pretty face, the fresh snowy skin. This was how things should be, this was marvelous, simply marvelous. Laying the rest of his hotdog down and looking away toward the idyllic pond, he closed his eyes briefly and prepared to give his answer.

CHAPTER 7

The Estate

Toward the end of September, Packard and Bradley dragged out the tarp cover for the pool and readied the heater for the gun range. They knew that Lancaster County weather could change overnight, and pushing winter preparations into October was like delaying a needed trip to the dentist. Bradley washed the SUV, his Corvette, then Coldgrave's Bentley, but not Bobbie Lee's camper, for she liked to do things herself.

"Hand me that cord," said Packard gruffly as the other took a moment to rest his back. They had dragged the heavy cover thirty feet from the shed and were almost to the pool.

"I think you're growling again, Len."

"Hand me the cord, sport, okay?"

Bradley yanked on the rope to pull some excess from the grommet, then held it out for the other to grasp. He didn't mind working with the man, for he liked him and often found himself resisting the impulse to emulate him. There was something about the old killer that appealed to him, whether because of his experience or simply his attitude. Just working beside the hard, grizzled man, who was never willing to risk being separated from his magnums, was inspiring.

"Len," he said as they stretched one corner over its hook, "could I ask you something a little personal? I mean, about somebody else?"

Packard looked at him suspiciously. "Why the hell not? Unless, of course, it's a pussy question—you know, sensitive and everything. Then I'm out. I'm not a sensitive guy, and I sure as goddamn hell don't want to be one, thank you very much."

He did not, of course, appreciate the man's profanity. It was not as bad as Gretchin's, but still it was a feature of their conversation he had constantly to overlook. Giving his nose a scratch, he said, "Uh, yeah, okay. Uh, so, what do you think about this team leader of ours?"

"Mary? She's great, bub."

"You don't think she's got an attitude—you know, posh wealth and all that?"

"What're you talking about, sport? No, I don't. She's great."

"Yeah, I suppose you're right. But, you know, she drinks so much, Len. I mean, come on."

"So what? She doesn't stagger when she shoots, right?"

"Yeah, but seriously, Len, don't you worry about her out on some project? Booze messes your reflexes up so much. I couldn't shoot at all if I drank as much as she does. I'd be totally wiped out."

"But she's not you, pal. She's never wiped out. It never even shows on her."

"It might. And then one of us could die in some silly gunfight, just because she's a split second late on the trigger or blurry on the aim. It could happen. We should be scientific about it, I think."

With a chuckle, "Scientific? Jesus. Look, you go fixin' her, and you could break her. And right now—she's great."

"Maybe we all like her, and everything, but a brain's still a brain, and alcohol's still alcohol. Don't you think she's an alcoholic?"

"Well, I drink—a lot sometimes. Over the years, I've heard that term just about too many times, I think. Did a little research on it once, just for my own dictionary, the one I carry in my head."

"And?"

"Well, putting it all together—society, science, my own experience—I just couldn't come up with a definition. So, I don't worry about it for myself."

"But what about on the projects?"

"Look, if I'm out on a job and I want a drink, I take it. If I don't, I don't. It's that simple, pal."

Momentarily, "Well, frankly, Mary's drinking scares me. I don't think it's right either."

The old killer stared at him. "Well, I see it the way your wife does, sport—I'm not a moralist. I simply don't care, and that's the best way to put it. I've got a simple view of life. I don't care who or what my enemies are, I just kill 'em. And I don't care who or what my friends are, I try to get along with them. And I try to stay clear of society. Society's simply a phenomenal plurality that someone took a shit in a long time ago. The only thing you can trust about society is that you can't trust it. Society's a mob, pal. But it sounds like you're getting a little complex about life, or you wouldn't have brought this up."

Bradley looked at the yellow teeth, the gritty eyes, but then replied, "Maybe."

The other gave a sniff, then a scratch at his chin. "But you know, if people need the term *alcoholism*, let 'em have it, it's okay with me. And if they want to be moral or religious about alcohol and close the bars on Sunday, I'm okay with it. I'll just stock up on Saturday and wait till the doors open on Monday."

"Okay, I can kind of see that."

"And," added Packard, "if some guy hits his wife, and all she can defend herself with is to say he's an alcoholic, that's great by me. I hate guys who do that—I'd cut their goddamn hands off. What I'm saying is that the term is there for a reason. Just let it go. But no, there ain't probably much science behind it. It's all just about people. And I don't like people much anyway."

"I kind of got that, yeah. ... Why don't you, exactly?"

With a shrug, "Why should I?"

"Okay, sure. But I do like people, Len, some of them are great. I could never cut myself off from everybody. ... You know, you say you're not a moralist, but you do moral things, you have to admit."

"Oh God! I suppose you're going to tell me that because I get rid of slimeballs, I help society, or something like that?"

"I don't know. I guess."

"Sure, pal, like, criminals can't be all bad, since they create police jobs."

"So, I guess you don't think much about politics or religion or anything like that."

"More bullshit. You've been thinking too much, pal, or watching too much TV." Then, straightening his back from the weight of the guns, he queried, "How's the wife?"

"Uh, fine, sure. I mean, she's kind of—the same. It's a little like being married to Margaret Hamilton, you know, but it's okay, I guess."

"Who's that?"

"She was the wicked witch of the west in the movie. You must have seen it, it's a really old movie."

Straightening his back again, "Thanks for poking at my age, sport, but no, I never saw your movie. I don't see many movies. Maggie likes them, so I see them with her. That Robert Mitchell's pretty neat sometimes, like in that moonshine movie."

"Oh, you mean Mitchum, sure."

With a shrug, "Who cares? Maggie didn't like it that much anyway. So, you're saying, Gretchin's like a witch?"

With a nod, "Kind of. I mean, sometimes."

"She's always seemed a little hard on you, I think everybody's got that down. But, she talks straight, and I like people that talk straight. It's the other ones you have to worry about. No, she may be a bitch, but she's no witch, bub. Besides, she's a pretty girl, you should be proud of her."

"I am, yes. Sure."

"Good."

"She's twelve years older than I am, you know."

"Does it matter?"

"I guess not."

"Sounds like you're not sure."

"No, really, the age thing doesn't matter."

"Hey, you'd better stay out of the movies, bub, you ain't a bit convincing."

With a chuckle, "You could be my psychiatrist!"

Packard scratched his whiskers. "Actually, if you need a psych, I'd recommend a good Jack Daniel's on ice. Or you could check your health plan and get the psychiatrist. But from what I hear, the whiskey's cheaper."

With a perfunctory grin, "I'm not old, but I'm old-school. I like things to be what they're supposed to be. And leaders are not supposed to be drunks. Or rich, with an elitist attitude."

"That may be right, bub. But I couldn't make myself care, if I tried."

"But I do, Len, I care a lot. I don't know why, but I care. I want to see Mary in a normal way, but I can't."

"You know what, it sounds like you might be jealous of her bub. Or maybe you're in love with her. I don't know, but something's wrong with what you're sayin'."

"Mary's gold, bub—pure gold."

Bradley looked at the rough, gray stubble, the wolfish, hunter's eyes, but did not reply.

"Maybe," said Packard, "my view's a little simple, but I like it that way. Life's cleaner that way, and it's the only way I could live anyway. Besides, with my view of things, I can drink the whiskey because I like it, not because I need it."

Then he got up, stretched his back again, and said. "Let's finish this job and pull some beers out."

Toward the end of October, following the evening meal, Coldgrave announced that she had heard from Willard that a new project had been assigned to the team. The particulars would be forthcoming as soon as he returned from Paris.

"It is my proposal that we toast the newlyweds," she offered, looking around at them. "I'll get a drink, and we can wish them well."

Maggie cleared her throat and smiled. "You already have a drink, Mary, you're holding it."

"Oh yes, of course. Well, then," and pushing from the table and standing, "I propose a toast. To Bob and Sandy, may they be happy all their days." And after they had all clinked glasses or bottles, she drained her glass and sat down.

"Well done, Mary," said Maggie. "So, they're coming back tomorrow? They seemed to make a good couple at the wedding, but I can't help wondering why everything happened so rapidly. I do wonder."

Gretchin gave a wry smile. "That's a little old-school, Maggie. Besides, I don't think Bob's the type to go beyond what's appropriate."

Packard blew across his coffee and agreed, "Nope."

"Well," returned Maggie, "they don't have much time, she's thirty-two."

Gretchin frowned, "Come on, thirty-two's nothing, they've got plenty of time. What I'm wondering is why they wanted to honeymoon in Paris. Any clues, Mary?"

Coldgrave shook her head, reaching for the bottle of Sapphire. "It is a place for lovers though, I can tell you that."

Everyone looked at her for this, and Bobbie Lee said, "Boy, I wouldn't touch that one with surgical gloves, Mary. Sounds like you're speakin' from experience. I've never even been to Paris."

Maggie raised her chin. "All I can say is, that must have been some picnic where they met."

"Sorry, Maggie," said Gretchin, "but Presbyterian picnics are nothing special, I've been to one and it was pretty dry. Did you see how tied-up those people were at the wedding? I couldn't live like that. Church tames you, doesn't it?"

Maggie smiled. "That seems to be one of the main reasons for church, yes."

"Some of the ladies were beautiful, weren't they? And not one of them had a tattooed ass, I'll bet."

"They were beautiful," agreed Maggie, "except for one or two, who looked like they'd eaten half the cake before they baked it. But it did seem to be a fairly well-to-do group."

Coldgrave wrinkled her nose. "Did it?"

"Well," said Maggie, "I think they made a very attractive couple. Sandy was as charming as you could get, I think, and Bob looked quite handsome, don't you think, Mary?"

Lowering the glass and giving a nod, "I'm sure he did, yes."

CHAPTER 8

A week later Willard arrived at the Estate. He and his driver took the usual place on the couch. Although Maggie and Gretchin both looked for Willard's body language to betray something of marital contentment, no one else seemed interested.

"So," said Willard as Connors and Bobbie Lee ambled in and leisurely took tea from the cart, "I am happy to report that Paris is an extraordinary place to spend one's honeymoon and the Eiffel Tower is as fun as ever. And on behalf of Sandy and myself, I want to thank you all for helping to make our wedding an unforgettable experience. Thank you all so very, very much. and the gifts, oh my goodness, what can I say—they were all, uh, very thoughtfully chosen, I'm sure." And bringing his hands together and nodding, he smiled upon the whole group.

Gretchin cleared her throat. "Did you like my gift?"

"I did, Gretchin, we both did, thank you so much."

"Because I didn't give one."

"Well, not everyone brought a gift, some gave us money."

"I didn't."

"Again," he returned, "that's just fine. We both appreciated it that you came and supported us. It just meant so much to us."

She cocked her head, "Actually, I'm kidding, we gave you a microwave."

His eyelids flickering, "I haven't had a chance to look at all the gifts, but I have no doubt that it will be perfect for us. Thank you, Gretchin, Bradley, we'll put it to good use."

"Bob," said Coldgrave, "you have a new project for us. Would you like to tell us about it?"

He sat back, thoughtful. "Yes, thank you, Mary. The new project concerns three individuals, three women, who have been on the Agency's radar for some time. They have been running a rather ingenious service, a kind of international murder connection business that links someone who wants someone else eliminated, with someone who will do it. The service actually provides competitive pricing, shopping around for the lowest-bidding assassin. They have been providing this service to foreign-based individuals, companies, and even governments. The business is cleanly run, so the problem is simply its popularity, or rather, that its popularity is damaging the reputation of the United States to the extent that the Agency feels it must, as a business, be eliminated, so to speak."

Gretchin sat forward. "It's an actual business, with books and bank accounts?"

"It seems so. It's not actually overt, it's hidden behind personal accounts. And books? Let's just say the Agency doesn't care. These people are not to be brought to justice, at least not before the courts. It's a fairly complex situation. The service is provided to plural entities and in fact links to plural entities, so the business operates on a pretty large scale. But none of that matters. The business is to be eliminated completely, cut off at the roots, as they say, which means that these three women have been made your targets."

Coldgrave put her glass down. "Intel? Oh, and where are these people?"

"Not much intel, I'm afraid, only a few photos, but they'll be useful. As to location, they're in Reading, not far from here actually."

Bradley grinned. "I don't know why, but I thought you were going to say somewhere exotic."

"Sorry, Bradley. Reading will have to do for now."

Gretchin looked at her husband. "That was pathetic, Bradley. No gold star, no nothing."

Turning away from her, "Stop picking."

"There is," said Willard, placing his hands together, "some danger involved. We believe they're armed and also have armed guards working for them."

"What level?" asked Bradley, an assertive expression on his face.

Gretchin looked at him, this man she had married, this Bradley Hopkins. Whenever he made a naive statement, he immediately tried to say something insightful. Whenever he spoke out of turn, he tried to clear himself by showing sensitivity. She had tried not to criticize him so much. She had even tried to love him.

Willard cleared his throat. "Well, Bradley, we're not sure. To be safe, you should consider them professionals. There are two of them, we think."

Showing her unease, Gretchin gave her head a shake and stuffed a wad of hair behind an ear. "That's cute," she said, "I love your *we think*, which means there might be more. What, couldn't cough up for a little more surveillance?"

Coldgrave crossed her legs. "What's the problem, Bob, with getting more intel?"

Here he glanced at the sidekick, then looked back at her. "The Agency doesn't want to risk loosing any surveillance people."

Gretchin squinted at him. "There's something you're not telling us."

"They've apparently killed at least two foreign agents just for snooping on the operation. It wasn't here, it was actually in India. But there were two separate incidents. The agents simply disappeared."

"So," said Bradley, "we shouldn't really consider these guards to be a couple of old bank cops."

"Correct."

"Are we talking about a compound situation?" queried Coldgrave.

He brightened, and after watching her lift the gin to her nose to breathe in its vapors, he replied, "No. And that's the good news—it's just a house, a very simple house. There are photos in the packet."

"Oh, good, good," said Gretchin, "then you probably won't need all of us on this one, right? Maybe just Kelly."

He looked at her, suppressing his anger at her disrespect. But it was ironic, he considered, that she should refer to Connors, for if in all the world there was indeed someone who could do the job alone, it was this Irish woman, this enigmatic, wraith-like killer of killers. "I don't think," he said at length, "that sarcasm helps, Gretchin, thank you. This is a very important project that has to be executed by this team. You would do well to be serious about it. I'm sure we would all appreciate that."

"Oh, sure," she returned, "I'm just worried that you're going to be so goddamn cheap on this one that you'll get us killed, too. Not that the Agency's *trying* to get us killed, or anything like that. Know what? I'll bet that if anything did happen to us, within ten minutes our profiles would be deleted and the paperwork shredded. You'd have to piss on the shredder motor to cool it down."

Bradley put both hands on top of his head in protest. "Jeez, Gretchin," he moaned, "that's a little rough. Bob's trying to do his best here. And the Agency's not being cheap, they're just working with a tight budget, that's all."

Glaring at him, "That's actually the way you see things, isn't it? You are so simple."

"Well, look at you," he retorted, "you're hopelessly pessimistic. You're against everybody and everything, such as Bob here or the Agency. You think everybody's out to cheat you. Bob said the Agency doesn't have a lot of money to throw around, that's all. I think you're the one that's simple."

"Go ahead, Bradley, just worship all of it."

Willard lifted his chin. "Gretchin, I wouldn't do anything that would hurt you or keep back anything that would help you, believe me. The Agency's not trying to get you or anyone else here killed. The team's safety is our first concern."

"Yeah," chimed Bradley, "so, stop picking on him, Gretchin."

Now her eyes grew fierce. "Fuck you, Bradley, twice! You know, if a mortician was pumping formaldehyde into you, you'd think you were getting a transfusion."

He watched as she got up and walked out of the room. When she was gone he said, "I think she'll be okay. No harm done, she'll be okay."

Willard said nothing further, but Maggie shook her head, and Bobbie Lee grinned. Coldgrave, her face expressionless, raised the glass to her lips, then drained it.

CHAPTER 9

Reading, Pennsylvania, November

The day began to take on a certain pallor as the SUV entered the exit. Bradley touched the brake as the vehicle began to sway. "Boy," he uttered, "all that ammo in the back doesn't make driving this cow easy."

"Yeah," returned Gretchin from behind Coldgrave, "so I guess we should've left the ammo home."

He gave the steering wheel a tap. "Funny, dear."

"Don't call me that. And don't complain either, just drive."

Beside him Coldgrave brought her mirror down and checked her lipstick. He glanced over as she tugged her shooting gloves up tighter, then flexed her fingers and balled up her fists. But then he felt Gretchin's eyes on him. This was not the first time he had noticed that she watched his response to other women. What did it matter whether he did or didn't look? No one, not even Gretchin, with her powers, could tell just exactly why he looked. He arched his back now and changed the position of his hands on the wheel. Still he could feel her eyes upon him, and he knew that she was calculating and would be remembering.

"This is an old town," he offered at length. "I think a lot of old people live here. Old bricks and old bones, right?"

Coldgrave, looked up from her map. "Do you see the motorcycle?"

"They're a few cars behind us, yeah. Just text them, Mary. Kelly watches her phone."

"Hey, Bradley," said Gretchin, "all the jobs we've been on, and you don't think we know Kelly watches her phone? You don't actually have to say stupid things, you know. And maybe Mary doesn't want to text them, okay? Don't tell people what to do, Bradley."

"Wow, you're right on cue, aren't you? Too bad you didn't bring a hammer, you could just hit me from behind."

Ignoring the exchange, Coldgrave said, "We should be there in a few minutes, so as long as you've seen them, I'll hold off for now."

"Good," he replied. Then to Gretchin, "See?"

Gretchin smirked. "See what, Bradley, see what, that she doesn't need your advice? Yeah, I can see that, dope. You don't seem to get it that you're not the team leader, Bradley. She knows what she's doing, you don't."

"So, you don't think I could be the team leader?"

"No."

As if wearied, Coldgrave looked out the window, but Packard, seated behind Bradley, growled, "Can't you two just shut the hell up?"

Bradley's eyes went to his mirror. "All right, they're right behind us now."

Coldgrave opened her phone and tapped out the message.

"Hope those tubes work okay," he said, glancing at the mirror again, "Kelly might need that M44 today. It was, like, a perfect fit, you should've seen it." And then, "Hey, I just got a thumb's up."

Coldgrave checked her phone, "Yes."

"There they go, they're breaking off."

They were in the city now, with rows and rows of brownstones lining the quaint streets. As there was minimal traffic, only minutes passed before they were in the same block as the targets' house.

Bradley leaned forward over the steering wheel to get a better look. "Look at these old places. I used to know a girl from here, a row house just like these. The ceiling in her's was, like, twelve feet or more, incredible." But Gretchin's voice came sharply, reminding him to keep his eyes on the street. Then he saw the motorcycle approaching from the opposite direction.

"Just move casually past the house," said Coldgrave, checking her purse for the .38 and the speedloaders. Then as they passed, "Two guards sitting on the front steps, smoking. Is that lucky, is that lucky?"

As the motorcycle passed them, Bradley said, "Kelly's seen them, too. Now they're turning the corner."

"Do the same."

He grinned. "Stick to the plan, right?"

Gretchin, pulling the Glock from her purse and racking it, said, "Yes, Bradley, the plan, you don't have to say that."

Packard reached into his sport coat, unsnapped one of the Smith's, then felt in his pocket for the speedloaders.

As Bradley turned the corner to circle the block, he said, "There were kids across the street, did you see that?"

"Yes," replied Coldgrave without emotion.

Uneasy, he turned another corner, then another, then the final one. The motorcycle, which had circled its own block, now again approached from the opposite direction.

"Oh, please," he muttered, slowing and pulling up a few doors from the house, "Kelly's got her helmet off and the carbine out. They're stopping in front of the house."

But of course Coldgrave had seen it, too. "All right, go, go now, we'd better cover the back alley. Hurry."

He obeyed, punching the accelerator and soon shooting them past the house.

But even as the SUV passed the stopped motorcycle, Connors, riding close up behind Bobbie Lee, brought the carbine over and took aim. Instantly one of the children playing on the sidewalk beside the motorcycle saw it and yelled for the others to run, then grabbed a little boy's hand and frantically began to drag him away. Then the gun went off, a fierce blast sounded, and a huge ball of yellow flame spread out from its muzzle. Desperately the girl grabbed up the boy and began to run.

Connors, confident she had blown a hole all the way through the guard's chest, deftly lifted the M44's bolt, pulled it, rammed the next round home, then fired again. This sequence happened so fast that the second guard only had time to watch his partner fall backward before he himself was also hit squarely in the chest.

"Goddammit, that thing's loud!" yelled Bobbie Lee, recoiling from the second blast. "Fuckin' Cossack gun!" But she looked just in time to see the man's collapsed body complete its bumpy slide down the steps and the cigarette fall from his lips.

Swinging her leg off the bike, Connors shoved the carbine back into the tube, pulled her .38 from her jacket, and started across the street toward the house. Bobbie Lee, hanging her helmet beside Connors', swung the kickstand out, left the engine running, and followed.

Stepping over the quickly forming pools of blood from the oozing bodies, Connors tried the front door, pulled it free and entered. Bobbie Lee, racking her P-64, was close behind her.

At the back entrance, Packard leveled the magnum and sent three blasts at the latch area, then pulled the door open. But even as he did, multiple pops were heard from inside. Then Coldgrave pushed her way past Packard, felt for the switch, and finally sent light into the basement. When the party reached the kitchen, just above them, they found Connors and Bobbie Lee standing over the bodies of the three targets. Stooping, Coldgrave looked into the dead faces of the women one by one. The heads of the corpses, shot multiple times, oozed and dripped blood. On one, only the gruesome socket of an eye remained.

"Anyone else here?" queried Coldgrave, shifting to avoid a run of blood.

"Didn't see anybody," answered Bobbie Lee, "jist these three, and of course the two guards out front dead as a stick. Wanna search the house?"

"No."

Wiping her nose on her sleeve. "It's prob'ly them, right?"

Coldgrave stood up and took a step back. "Well, it certainly looks like them. I suppose it's them."

Connors, who had reloaded, shoved the gun back into her jacket, then pulled a knife from her jeans and snapped it open. "Want an ear?"

Gretchin blurted, "Jesus, Kelly, put that away."

But Coldgrave merely replied, "No, I don't want an ear, it's probably them." And turning for the door to the basement, "All right, let's go, everyone out. See you at home. Text me when you're out of the city. Come on, let's go."

When they had cleared the city limits and heard from Connors that they too were on the open road, Coldgrave put in the call to Willard. "Yes, hi, Bob. Just letting you know the project's completed. . . . Everything's fine, yes. . . . No, no one hurt. . . . All right, thanks. Talk to you later. . . . Right, bye." Then she dropped the phone back into her purse and pulled her visor down. Removing her right glove, she touched the corner of her mouth with a finger. Then she tugged the glove back on and pushed the visor up.

"Ever get lipstick on your gloves?" Bradley asked as he switched lanes to pass a truck.

After a moment, "I've never thought about it, Bradley. What would it matter?"

"Yeah," chimed Gretchin, fastening her eyes on him, "what would it matter, Bradley?"

"Oh, just asking. I'll bet you those gloves cost fifty dollars—make that a hundred."

"God," said Gretchin, "what do you expect her to say? You know she doesn't know how much they cost, stooge."

"No," said Coldgrave, looking out her window at the fields, "I actually don't."

"I know, I know," he came back, "you throw a credit card at everything except the big things, like your Bentley, and those you simply order through your lawyer. I know. I just like talking about it. All that money. I'll bet you don't even know how much you have, right?"

With a sigh, "Correct."

"I'll bet it's not millions, I'll bet it's a billion dollars. Wow, that boggles my mind."

Coldgrave did not respond, but Gretchin did. "Bradley, why don't you just shut your mouth and drive the goddamn car." And as this only made him grin, she said, "Mary, I apologize for him."

But he staged a broader grin and said, "You apologize for me? Wow, that's insulting. But you're good at that, aren't you? You could probably teach it at the college level, maybe to seniors."

She did not bother to look at him now, but like Coldgrave, merely looked out her window. "If you ever get out of high school, Bradley," she said, "you could be a nice guy. But you're stuck there, aren't you? You're really, really stuck there."

CHAPTER 10

The Estate

Bobbie Lee lowered the weights to the posts as Connors closed the door, then threw herself onto the bed and stretched out. "Good thing you're always welcome here," she drawled, grasping the bar again to bench-press the weights, "you might git yoursilf shot walkin' in like that."

Grabbing a magazine, then watching as the weights were pressed, "You ever t'ink of doin' the bodybuildin' stuff?"

Following three presses, "No, thank you, I don't want to lose my agility at ridin' 'n shootin'. I'm lithe, and people who git into big-time liftin' ain't lithe."

"T'en why do et at all?"

Bobbie Lee sat up, puffed her cheeks, then reached for the hand exerciser. "I need to stay in shape to handle the bike. Harley's are heavy machines. How would you like ridin' on the back of that thing and doin' our escapades with me at the tiller, if I was skinny?"

Connors lowered the magazine and let her eyes run over the forearm muscles as the hand exerciser was squeezed and released. "You're not skenny."

The other counted off fifty squeezes, then shifted the device to the other hand. "Yeah, well, I don't want to git skinny or fat, girl. . . . You sound bored. Wanna watch the fights? UFC's on tonight. Come on, lit's watch. Maybe Holly Holm'll be on."

Turning another page, "How many of t'ose do you do a day?"

"This hand thing? I do about fifty with each hand four times a day."

"T'at's two hundred a day weth each hand."

"I know, I went to school. It's for shootin' and ridin'. I toldya, girl, a Harley's a goddamn horse."

"Wesh I had your muscles."

"Don't worry, I'd trade my muscles for your tits any day of the year, girl. . . . So, what say, watch some TV?"

Connors turned another page, but did not respond.

"Hey, you ain't gittin' all sad on me, are you? Remimber that time in Cape May, when you started gittin' all melancholy and there wasn't nothin' to git melancholy about? There was boats, there was seafood, there was beautiful weather, and we got to kill, what, four people? We even got to play mini'ture golf, remimber that? And you almost ruined it by gittin' sad, and ever'thing."

"Et was noice there, loike."

"Lord, I could've eaten them motorboats, they were so pritty. And the shrimp—remimber the shrimp? Bigger'n my hand. Boy, that was great. Boy, those were times. Great mim'ries."

Toward the end of November Willard called Maggie to decline her invitation for Thanksgiving, since he and Sandy had committed to the holiday dinner at church. He suggested instead that just he come for a visit sometime in December, as he had a new project to discuss. When Maggie countered with the Saturday before Thanksgiving as everyone was anxious to greet his new bride, he accepted.

"I assume," said Gretchin after dinner one evening, "that Sandy's been cleared?"

"She has, yes," replied Coldgrave. "Not that I trust the Agency to vet anyone properly, but we'll have to take them at face value, I'm afraid."

"Yeah," returned Gretchin sarcastically, "and how many times have we taken their intel at face value only to find out it was worthless? Face value can get you both screwed and killed."

"Very true," said Coldgrave, "but at least we'll be able to see how much of his Agency work Bob is willing to reveal to Sandy. Besides, we shall all enjoy a wonderful Christmas dinner together."

Maggie cleared her throat. "Mary, this will be Thanksgiving, Christmas is the next one."

"Oh yes, of course, the one coming up is the one with the tree."

"No," replied Maggie, "Thanksgiving's with the turkey, the next one is Christmas, with the tree."

"Right, of course." And tilting her drink toward Maggie, "I'm looking forward to both of them. . . . But when do they bob for apples in the tub of gin?"

Bradley, cutting into his pie, nearly choked. "You use gin? I can't believe it. That must cost a fortune."

Coldgrave gave him a blank look, then queried, "What do you use?"

"Water, right out of the garden hose."

"Do you drink it afterward as part of the fun? Apples make gin taste so divine."

As he simply stared at her, Gretchin said, "They usually bob for apples at Halloween, Mary."

Coldgrave smiled. "Yes, of course."

Maggie merely blinked and adjusted the teapot to be more symmetrical with the cookies. Daintily she smoothed her hair back and looked over at Coldgrave. How was it that anyone so beautiful and glamorous could be so out of touch with such things as commonly observed holidays? She let her eyes run over the expensive, well-cut clothes. Certainly the little boots alone must have cost at least a thousand dollars. How many high-society Christmas parties had she attended, how many holiday-appropriate party dresses had she worn, how many gallons of Nolet's had she consumed at those parties, and yet still she could not consistently distinguish between Christmas and Halloween, or Thanksgiving and New Year's, or distinctly know when any other holiday was taking place? Were the rich completely out of touch with reality, or was it just this particular woman, this gorgeous show piece of style and glamour? Such disparity was annoying at best. And as she looked Maggie again, perhaps this time self-consciously, smoothed her hair back. She had let it grow following her marriage to Packard, so that now it was well below her shoulders. And if there were moments when she wondered whether a return to her traditional Presley cut might be advantageous, overall she had grown comfortable with what her husband considered a more glamorous look. But if she were to become as wealthy and well dressed as this woman, whom admittedly she admired so much and felt so close to, she at least could never allow herself to confuse the holidays.

"Tomorrow?" said Willard as he accelerated to pass a Mennonite wagon. "That would be too soon, don't you think? You'll only be getting to know them today. What, did you exchange maybe three words with them at the wedding?"

She tried as they passed to see the eyes of the mother and father driving the wagon. "It could be fun," she said, facing front again, "and I really think I'll like them. I practically know them now, you've described so much about them."

"I don't think you'll like them at all after you've been around them for very long."

"Why, for heaven's sake?"

His hands fidgeting with the heater dial, "They're strange, eccentric."

"You've said that, and I can't get what you mean. I know strange people, so what? I know eccentric people too."

With a patient tone, "Let's just see how it goes today. Then we'll talk about it on the way home."

"Well, I want to have them over, whether we have them tomorrow or not."

"Tomorrow's too soon, it doesn't even sound right. Please, let's just see how it goes, okay?"

Turning into the long drive, he deliberately said nothing, but let her get her own feel for the place. After rounding the fountain, he said, "All their cars are over there in the old stables. One's a Bentley Continental—half a million bucks probably, I kid you not." When there was no response he added, "And there's a Harley Davidson motorcycle." And bringing their sedan to a stop at the front door, "Pretty crazy, huh?"

Following greetings, Maggie and Gretchin took Sandy away for a tour of the house, while Bradley and Packard grabbed Willard for a game of pool. Coldgrave, who had gone to New York, was due to return in time for the afternoon briefing and dinner.

For most of the walk through the two houses, Sandy seemed to take things in stride, in spite of encountering nearly every kind of weapon used on the team's projects. The strong odor of gun cleaning fluid emanating from Packard's maintenance room did not repel her, and Bobbie Lee's Confederate flag only elicited a chuckle. Upon entering the recreation and reading room, she seemed even to be somewhat charmed as her husband halted mid-shot, leaned upon his cue, and remarked, in a very old-school way, how pretty the ladies were.

The only irregularity in the tour was when they came to Connors' room, where she spun round on them half naked, sporting a new bra holster she had been experimenting with before a mirror.

As neither Gretchin nor Maggie took any notice of the situation, Sandy, somewhat aghast, queried meekly whether they were interrupting anything and suggested they might come back later. Without a word, Connors nonchalantly yanked the revolver from the bra, then tossed it to her. The gun was deftly caught, its cylinder rolled out, the primers of its five cartridges were inspected, and the cylinder was snapped back into place, all in a few seconds. When the piece was held out butt-first, Connors stepped forward and closed her hand upon its grip, making a point to insert her finger into the trigger guard. As a final comment, her face expressionless, her eyes upon Sandy, she simply shoved the gun back into the holster, as if to say that at least now they were all aware that Willard's quiet little wife was not exactly ignorant of weapons.

For her part, Sandy, her eyes upon the ample breasts and the holstered gun between them, merely offered, "That's quite an outfit, Kelly. Nice to see you again."

"Roight, same here," replied Connors simply, giving her nose a quick wipe with the back of her hand.

CHAPTER 11

When they were seated in the living room and Maggie had rolled in the tea cart, Willard asked Coldgrave, who had just gotten in from New York, if Connors was coming to the briefing.

"She'll be here," she replied, her eyes upon the cart to see if Maggie had brought her gin, "she's rather independent, you know."

Bobbie Lee swallowed her mouthful of beer and added, "Most of us are."

And Gretchin, picking a piece of lint from her low-cut sweater, added, "Don't look at me, I'm not independent, I'm now just an obedient housewife who tries to do what she's told." Then she threw a look at Bradley, who gave them all a roll of his eyes.

"So," said Willard, glancing at his watch, "How does everyone like our new president? Did we all vote?"

Maggie smiled pleasantly. "Religion and politics, Bob, are pretty much ignored around here."

He looked around at them. "But you must have voted."

Bobbie Lee swallowed another gulp of beer. "Killy can't vote, need you ask why?"

"Yes, but the rest of us are citizens."

Grumpily, Packard said, "I voted for more ammunition, think I'll get it?"

"Well, yes, Len, I do."

"Good, that's what I wanted to hear, pop."

Then Connors strode in and took a seat beside Bobbie Lee.

"Beer?" queried Bobbie Lee.

Getting up again, "No, but I'll take some of Maggie's black stuff and one of tham fuckin' cookies."

But Maggie was already up. "Now, now, Kelly, sit down, I'll get your tea, it's my special blend today. And a chocolate chip?" After getting these for her, Maggie left for the kitchen, a few moments later returning with Coldgrave's drink. "Sorry, Mary, I had left it on the counter. Sapphire okay?"

Willard, growing impatient, leaned forward, but clearly unwilling to say anything to Connors for being late, put his hands together, and said, "Can we get down to business, would that be okay?"

Gretchin clacked her cup and saucer, as if to point out that he had spoken out of turn. "Mary," she said, "what do you think, would you like to start things now?"

He stared at her. "Gretchin, I just said that."

Narrowing her eyes, she replied icily, "We usually wait for Mary to start things. You know that, I think."

He could not help recoiling from the rebuke and felt Sandy stiffen at the obvious insubordination, but he did not reply.

Coldgrave, who had been busy inhaling the alcohol vapors from her glass of iced gin, looked up. "Yes, of course," she returned, "that would be fine, Gretchin, surely. Bob, you have a new project for us, is that correct?"

Taking a moment to regain his composure, he said, "All right, yes, everyone, I do have a project, yes. But first, I would like to discuss the Reading project. There were some anomalies that we need to talk about, things that were not quite kosher, if you know what I mean." He looked around to discern their reaction, but finding only blank expressions, continued, "It turns out that you were observed by—"

"By whom?" interrupted Gretchin.

"Well, by children. I mean, seriously, don't you think you could have been more discreet? Your activities were called in to the police by a lot of people, as a matter of fact. You were aware of people there, correct? There were a number of pedestrians outside and parents and children in the library."

"I shot cheldran?" queried Connors with surprise. "I dedn't shoot any keds."

"No, no, of course not, Kelly," he returned, "I didn't mean that. But I understand that you opened fire in front of children playing on the sidewalk—right beside you."

"So?"

He could not suppress a chuckle of painful incredulity. "What do you mean, *so*? You can scat children for life that way, I'm sure you're aware of that."

Gretchin rolled her eyes, "Anything else, Bob? You said anomalies, plural. So, what else?"

Sandy cleared her throat in an obviously complaining tone, as if to communicate not only to Willard but indeed to everyone that the remark had been disrespectful.

"Well," he stammered, "did you have to shoot the guards right on the front steps? Was that judicious?"

Then Bradley spoke up, "I did point out the children to Mary. I was a little concerned about that myself."

Willard shot him a grateful look. "Well, that's what I mean, that's being judicious, that's good. And what did she say to that?"

"She just said that she had seen them."

As the others watched in silence, Coldgrave merely lifted her glass and casually took a sip of the iced gin.

"Mary?" said Willard. "You saw them?"

"Yes. They were playing on the sidewalk."

"Well?"

"Well what? I decided to execute the plan. The guards were sitting there like, *shoot us, please*, and I decided to execute the plan. It was a good plan, it worked, like a German watch, isn't that what they say?"

Maggie cleared her throat. "Um, Swiss watch, Mary, I think they say it that way."

"Okay," put in Gretchin impatiently, "anything else, Bob?"

He stared at her, his mouth open, as if in disbelief. "Uh, well—" Here he looked back at Sandy, pain in his face. But as she merely folded her arms, he simply closed his mouth.

"Bob," said Bradley, letting go of his shoestring, "isn't there anything more to say about the children?"

Willard swallowed, then replied, "I—I do wish that everyone could try to be a little more judicious when it comes to the public. Lots of care has to be taken to avoid executing projects in front of the public, especially when children are nearby. That is not an unreasonable request, I think." Here he looked at Connors. "Kelly? Yes?"

Connors wiped her nose on her sleeve. "Sher."

He smiled. "Good. . . . Well, I think we can go on, then, to the briefing for the next project. There has been a problem with a certain country that doesn't love us."

"I know," put in Gretchin, "you want us to guess. But then, which ones do love us, exactly?"

He looked back at Sandy. He was beginning to wish he had not brought her. His hope that her presence would elicit respect from them was gone. Momentarily he replied, "You're right, Gretchin, not many of them do. In any case, one of our agents was caught by a drug group in that country. They turned her over to the authorities, believe it or not. She was brutally interrogated and then left in her cell without care. There she died. The Agency wishes to answer the action." He paused to clear his throat. "We have received information that five of their diplomats plan to visit New York City next week. We have no idea why they're coming. They will be arriving in Philadelphia via commercial air. That's as much as we know for certain about the travel, except that they've booked the return flight, also out of Philly. Apparently they plan to get to New York by car. Of course, it could be by train or even bus, who knows? But they must not be allowed to reach New York. Not because of their business there, which, again, we don't know, but—" Here he stopped, with an unhappy sigh. "Do you think you, uh," and here he looked around at them, "do you think the team can handle it?"

Bobbie Lee took a swig from her beer, then queried, "How do you mean?"

"Well," he replied, obviously unhappy, "these guys, uh, had nothing to do with the agent's death, nothing at all."

She grinned at him. "You mean it's strictly vengeance. Hot damn!"

He looked at her, making no attempt to hide his sadness.

She tilted the bottle toward him. "But you don't like it, do you? It's eatin' at your guts, right?"

"I'm a little uncomfortable with it, certainly. But I understand the dynamics, so I'll work through it."

Still grinning, "Guess you're gonna have to git the advice of the elders and say some prayers over this one, huh?"

When he slumped back against the couch cushions Sandy simply reached out and laid a hand on his knee.

Connors, clearly bored, here got up, pulled a bottle of beer from the cart's ice bucket and sat down again. She handed it to Bobbie Lee, who snapped open her utility knife, removed the cap, and handed it back. Giving the rim a wipe with her sweatshirt, Connors tipped the bottle up and let it chug.

"Probably no rifles on this one," offered Packard. "Five of them, maybe more, right? And in a car or whatever."

Coldgrave finished her gin. "Well, I would take one along. You know, Kelly, the velocity of that 7.62x54 you use means virtually zero drop at a hundred yards. It's a wonderful round. I remember once—"

"Mary," put in Maggie gently, "can I just refresh that for you?"

Handing her the glass, "Yes, of course, Maggie, thank you, you're way ahead of me."

Gretchin, who had not taken her eyes off Willard, said, "Did you ever think, Bob, of going into the ministry? I mean, full-time, instead of part-time like this?"

Ignoring the insult, he smiled at her, his brow unfurrowing. "Actually, yes. But I'm pretty sure it wouldn't have worked out."

"How so? You seem so—perfect for it."

Another smile. "You're not the only one to say that, Gretchin. But actually I'm not that good at speaking, and you have to be able to speak well, people expect it."

Tipping her bottle toward him, Connors offered sympathetically, "I don't speak well mesalf, Bob."

CHAPTER 12

Following the evening meal, Maggie set a cold blueberry pie on the table, then brought in a pot of her darkest tea. She was glad to have Sandy as their guest for something besides the briefing, as the team almost never entertained anyone other than Agency people. But the tears started as she thought of Martina, how she would have loved this. But then Packard caught it and laid his hand upon her arm.

Gretchin also caught the moist eyes. Noting Packard's comforting gesture, she wondered whether her own husband would do the same. She looked at Sandy, then at Willard.

"Maggie," Willard said with a smile of satis- action, "again that was a great meal. I love Cornish hen. The vegetables, they tasted right out of the ground. And now this wonderful pie. Sandy and I both love blueberry pie."

"Glad you liked it, Bob," she replied simply. Oh, how much she would give to retrieve the past, to bring back Martina and live again the life they had together. She missed so much the simple course of each day, with the teaching together, the sharing of achievements and trials, the shopping, the coming home to their little house in Lawncrest for dinner, the reading of the newspaper, and the chatting. Even the work with the advisory team, as it was then. . . . Oh the memories, how real, how visceral they had become for her.

"Yes, Maggie," chimed Sandy, "Bob says everything you make is so delicious he can barely stop eating it. He says he'd be fat if he lived here, and I can see why. And everything's so beautiful too, you must have an artistic side."

With a little wave, Maggie pulled the dish closer and reached for the knife. "Now, who would like pie, and who is for tea, and who for coffee?"

"I thought you said Mary was the alcoholic," said Sandy as they drove home that night.

"She is."

"They're *all* alcoholics, Robert. I've never seen people drink so much."

"Well, trust me, she can drink the rest of them under the table."

"I think she was drunk, I'm sorry."

"I have never seen her actually drunk. She just doesn't get drunk, that's all. She's obviously an extremely highly functioning alcoholic."

"I was glad Maggie only had wine, I didn't feel so alone."

He glanced over at her. He loved her profile, even in the dark. Since the day at the picnic he had not stopped wanting to look at her. What was it about things you looked at and just had to look again and again? "But quite a group," he said, "right?"

"*Group*?" she repeated, astonished. "Somehow that word just isn't enough. You know that Mr. Packard is crazy, don't you? And Bobbie Lee was like someone out of a Civil War movie, or a carnival. Oh, and Kelly Connors, really? Do you know, she tossed me a loaded gun in her room? We walked in on her, and there she was, half naked, and she pulled her gun out and tossed it to me with no warning whatever."

"What did you do?"

"I swung the cylinder out, looked at the primers, closed it up, and handed it back grip-first, the way you're supposed to do."

Giving her another glance, "Where did you learn that?"

"I'm not ignorant, Robert. I know about guns. And do you know what she did? She deliberately put her finger on the trigger as she took it back."

"What did you do?"

"Nothing, just acted nonchalant as I could about it."

"Well—there you go, then, you're all set to deal with these people."

"But these are psychotic people, Robert, you should be careful."

Putting a forefinger up, "Well, a person has to have a certain type of mentality just to be able to do this kind of work, you have to understand that. It's like an equation, where not everybody has the suitable combination of factors to get a certain answer. Actually, the guy who formed the team, a guy named Kessler, had a theory that he could make anybody into an assassin. According to him, the important variable was the circumstances you surrounded someone with."

"*Someone* being *anyone*?" she returned. "Somebody like you or me?"

"Right, exactly." And with a chuckle, "Want to be an assassin?"

"That's not funny, Robert, don't even say things like that. It's really gross to think about, I could never do that kind of work."

"Well, the Agency didn't exactly buy that part of his theory. They did let him test the other part of his theory, that amateurs could be sometimes more innovative than professional agents. To a certain extent he proved himself right. But I think he sort of stacked the deck by mixing professional killers with amateurs who were just a little bit off. And I think the factor of luck was not given the weight it should have been given when his theory was judged to be correct. This team has been exceptionally, almost inexplicably lucky. . . . In any case, that was the team. Quite theatrical, huh?"

"You know they're dangerous, right?"

"Oh sure, I do, yes. But you have to cut them some slack. The work just wouldn't get done, otherwise. And it's important work, it's for the government, the country."

Through the windshield she watched as the highway seemed to roll toward them. But life was like that, she considered, it often seemed to be coming toward you when in reality you were going toward it. It sometimes seemed to be giving you things, when in reality it was taking things away. It was odd, she mused, how deceptive life could be, yet you were forced by circumstances and your own limitations to trust it.

Then she said, "Mary's certainly the rich one, like you said. Did you see those clothes, do you know what they cost?"

As if such a thing was of little interest to him, "Not the foggiest, I'm afraid."

She looked at him as he drove, his hands on the wheel, his eyes on the highway. "But you did seem to notice them."

"Well, I did, yes."

"She's attractive, isn't she?"

Cautiously, "She is, yes."

"Well, I don't think she knows how much her clothes cost, either. She had no idea what the boots cost. I asked her—that's right, I simply asked her. Actually I knew, at least round about, but I asked her anyway. She just didn't know."

"How much did they cost? Actually I didn't even notice she had boots on."

"That's good, Robert. I wouldn't want you noticing too much about her. She's really, really pretty. So, just don't go seeing too much there, okay?"

"Well, I said I didn't notice the boots."

"I know. But if you do notice, don't go looking above the boots. She's quite—sexy. . . . The boots probably cost between five and ten thousand dollars. How much is she worth?"

"No idea."

"Oh, come on, please tell me. Women want to know these things. Just tell me."

"No one knows. I'm sure she doesn't."

Momentarily, "You haven't told me that much about your work, you know."

"It's sort of secret, it has to be, I told you that."

"But I want to be a part of your work, so I can be more a part of your life. You can trust me, Robert, I will keep your secrets. Please—let me into your world. I can check your blindspots, although I'm sure you don't have many, or any, probably."

He said nothing to this, but simply gave his mirrors a check and then looked out through the windshield at the traffic.

CHAPTER 13

Philadelphia International Airport

Coldgrave ran through the photos again, then looked up at the crowds of holiday travelers. "The windshield is very dusty," she said.

Bradley stiffened. "Sorry, I was going to clean it, but didn't get the chance."

"Right," said Gretchin from the back, "you were so rushed, Bradley, sure, we understand."

"Sarcasm is not good," he returned, "even though you're so good at it."

"You're pretty good at making excuses."

"Don't start a fight, please don't."

"Well, look at the windshield, idiot. And my window here, look at this—filthy. How're we supposed to identify these people, for God's sake? This isn't an army tank, it's supposed to be a nice car with clear windows, dope."

"I said I was sorry."

"Oh, you're sorry," she shot back, "that makes the windows clear, doesn't it?"

"How do things get so dusty?" muttered Coldgrave, as if to herself.

Bradley smirked, "There's too much dust in the world, right?"

"Don't be sarcastic to her, jerk," said Gretchin angrily, "you can talk like that to me, but not to Mary. Be respectful, you fucking jerk."

"O-oo, her feathers are up," he teased. "My wife is mad, I'd better watch it."

Then Packard asked, "Mary, what's the chance these cranks had to take different flights?"

"I've asked Bob that, and he's just texted back negative. They're all coming in together, and they're here now, so eyes open, everyone."

"Well," said Gretchin, "thanks to Bradley here, we might get to *see* the wrong guys."

Bradley slapped the steering wheel. "Stop, Gretchin, stop, just stop."

Then Coldgrave said, "I've got them, just out the door. See them?"

Bradley pulled the shift down. "Tell me when."

"Hold it," she returned. "What's that, a scout troop or something? Look at that. I guess that won't do, especially after Bob's lecture the other day."

Gretchin, stretched to see. "Uh, those are nuns, Mary."

"Oh. Okay, then I think we're good to go."

Gretchin cleared her throat. "No, Mary, why don't we wait. That would be worse than shooting with kids around. You can't chance hitting a nun."

"They're Catholic, correct?"

"Yes, Roman Catholic. They're the ones with the pope and everything."

"Okay, maybe you're right. Stand down, Bradley."

Shifting the lever up, he turned and shot Gretchin a grateful look. Then he said, "That's a cab. Those guys aren't going to take a cab to New York, I hope. Jeez, that would cost a mint. No way."

They followed the cab through the first turn, which was to the left, then to the right, which led into to a car rental facility. With the SUV's engine running, they watched as the men, who had crammed into the front and rear seats, got out and pulled their meager luggage from the cab's trunk.

"Why are they slapping each other and laughing like that?" queried Bradley.

"Shut up, Bradley," returned Gretchin.

But he could not help commenting how wasteful it had been for them to take the cab such a short distance and that they must be bilking their guys back home. She told him again to shut up, then looked at her phone and said, "Kelly's checking for a go."

But Coldgrave said, "Tell her it should be a few minutes yet, they've gone in to secure the rental. . . . Bradley, shut it down."

He obeyed, and everyone relaxed.

Coldgrave pulled the .38 from her purse, held it for a moment in her gloved hand, then returned it. "You know," she said, "there are so many configurations now for .38 Special compared to a few years ago, but there's still nothing for easily penetrating a car door. It's a shame, because it's such a nice round."

Packard, who had nearly spat at this, said, "Then why not get a gun?"

A chuckle. "Yes, Mr. Packard, only a magnum's a gun, right? But with a .38 I'm not sacrificing facility for power. And I want that muzzle to stay more on target for the second shot. But then, you knew that. You magnum people always have to make the case for power."

"You're the one that complained the .38 wouldn't go through a car door. All I'm saying is that I complained, too, until I got a magnum. That was a long time ago, and I didn't look back."

Coldgrave touched her nose delicately with a gloved forefinger. "I guess I'm looking for a trade-off, a little more power than a P+ and maybe a pointed titanium jacket and half an inch more to the barrel."

"Sorry, Mary, it's not going to happen. Just get a nine, if you want a trade-off."

"I'm afraid I'm quite sold on the reliability of a revolver, and I don't care for cut cylinders or moon clips."

Impatiently, "Well, I guess you're stuck, then. And I guess I'll always have a job, since you'll need me to get through that door when you can't. Give me penetration every time."

With a chuckle, Gretchin put in, "Why do men like to use that word?"

Ignoring this, he added, "Osipov liked his Tokarev because it would go through level-three body armor. He said if the KGB had a car chase, they always pulled out the Tok. But for close-up, you're right, they would use the Makarov for it's facility and rapid fire in a gunfight."

Bradley lifted his chin. "You miss him, Len?"

With a sigh, "Not really, bub. I don't miss people."

"He liked guns, but he liked cameras more."

"Yeah, he was sensitive. Poor guy. Yeah, he liked cameras more. And he liked Martina more than anything in all the universe. Poor guy."

"There is," said Coldgrave, "something beautiful, almost human, about a gun, something organic."

"Well," returned Packard, his fingers moving over the speedloaders in his pocket, "I never thought of a gun as organic, but I can see that, Mary, yeah. Hey, you should write a book."

Giving the steering wheel a drum with his fingers, Bradley said, "I see guns as machines. I've loved machines since I was a kid."

"Oh," returned Gretchin, "and how long's that been?"

The inevitable exchange was cut short when Coldgrave pushed her sunglasses on and said, "Okay, that's them. Maybe they left through a side door. They've pulled the car back to the front to get their luggage. My, that was lucky." And as Bradley started the engine, "All right, Gretchin, tell Kelly it's a go. They're in a silver minivan, we're following them now."

Once on the freeway, Bradley dropped the SUV back to a three-car lag and pressed the sprayers and wipers into service. A minute later, the motorcycle appeared in his mirror.

"You've only smeared it," said Gretchin. "Thanks again, Brad."

He felt his neck tighten. "It'll clear, don't worry, give it a minute."

"And where would we get this minute?"

But Coldgrave said, "That's all right, I think we'll just follow them awhile. Get it clean, Bradley."

Then Gretchin said, "Another text. Kelly's waiting for a go."

Bradley glanced at the mirror. "Yeah, they're right behind us. Boy, Kelly's a pusher, isn't she? Guess she likes being the first bullet out of the gun."

Coldgrave gave her head a quick shake. "Tell her to definitely wait for now, we're just following."

"You don't think they'll pick us up?" queried Bradley.

She looked over at him. "They're diplomats, not spies. We'll be fine. Just follow them, and, Gretchin, make sure Kelly gets that straight. Get a confirmation, read it to me."

Gretchin tapped out the message, sent it, then muttered, almost to herself, "Look at all this traffic."

Bradley gave a congruent nod. "Holiday stuff."

Glancing at the phone, "Kelly's just texted *okay.*"

"I expect," said Coldgrave, "these guys will have to pull in for a restroom. They're older."

If he could have stared at her, he would have. "Hey, yeah, the prostate. You're sharp, Mary."

But then instantly he felt Gretchin's eyes upon him for this. It always had to be there, the power of her eyes, the searching of her scrutiny, menacing him, making him feel smallish, deficient, even criminal. What an awful thing marriage had turned out to be. He hated being judged for his natural impulses. What was wrong if he wanted to compliment Mary or look over at her as she went into her purse or checked her gun? All right, it had been more than that on a few occasions. But Mary was odd, exotic, and it was only natural to want to look at something exotic. And even if secretly he had wished to see more of Mary's body, what was wrong with that? He could almost smell her lipstick sometimes as she put it on. Life was too complex, just too darned complex. Then he heard Gretchin's voice.

"Keep your eyes on the road, Bradley," she warned. "We can't lose them."

"I am, Gretchin," he returned defensively, "I am." Had he unconsciously glanced at Mary's legs? Surely he had not.

Then Gretchin looked over at Packard, at the lines in his face. "What're you thinking about, Len?"

With a melancholy chuckle, "The good old days, I guess. ... Actually I'm thinking how it must be cold as hell for them back there on that bike."

She looked out her window. "You might worry about Kelly, but not Bobbie Lee. I saw her take out on that motorcycle the other day in just a T-shirt. She's crazy."

"The outdoor type, that's all. No, she's not crazy."

The way he said this made her look over at him again. Then she looked at Bradley as he drove and let her mind go back for a moment to other times.

CHAPTER 14

"There's a rest stop," said Bradley suddenly. "Okay, let's see if you're right, Mary."

Indeed the minivan did take the exit, as did the SUV and the motorcycle. Bradley waited for the minivan to park, then pulled into a space four cars away. The motorcycle pulled up across the lane behind the SUV.

Slowly the doors of the minivan were opened, and the targets piled out and began to saunter toward the restrooms. But then Bradley caught Connors' form in his mirror as she dismounted, handed her helmet to Bobbie Lee, and began to follow the men.

"Oh, please," he moaned, "Kelly's following them. Oh my, not here. Look at all these people. Not here, please not here."

Coldgrave whirled in her seat, saw Connors, then got out.

"Kelly!" she called. And when she had caught up, "What are you doing?"

With a shrug, "Not'in', joost goin' to pee."

"I'll bet."

"Joost goin' to pee, Mary."

"In the women's?"

A mischievous look. "I t'ought I'd try the men's."

Sternly, "Not here, not in the restroom. They're not armed. We could do it when they get in the car, but not in the restroom—it would be extremely injudicious."

Momentarily Connors gave a reluctant nod, turned, and walked back to the motorcycle.

When Coldgrave had returned to the SUV, she said simply, "She was going to do it."

With a groan, Bradley let his eyes go shut. "Look at all these families. She's nuts, she's just plain nuts. Boy, that's a thirst for blood."

Growing uncomfortable, Gretchin shifted in her seat. "Turn the heat up, Bradley, it's cold back here."

But Coldgrave put in, "Gretchin, text Kelly, *in car here, it's a go*, do it now. And, Bradley, when they're near their car, back out, and when they're inside, block them."

He was incredulous. "But there are families here, Mary," he pleaded, "look at them. And look at all the kids, look. You can't do this."

Ignoring him, she reached into her purse for the .38, while Packard drew out one of his magnums and Gretchin frantically tapped out the message. Then she said, "Bradley, you stay in the car with Gretchin. Len, I'll need you. Gretchin, did she confirm?"

"Yes, confirmed."

"All right, here they come. Back it out, Bradley." As he obeyed and backed them from the spot she turned to glimpse the motorcycle as it began to roll. "Okay," she said, "and when that last door shuts, pull up and block them."

One of the men, however, who had removed his jacket, began to laugh as he dropped it to the pavement. Slowly he picked it up as another minivan pulled into the adjacent space. Continuing to laugh, he got in and pulled the door shut.

"Hold it," commanded Coldgrave, "just hold it. That looks like a mother with kids in there."

Immediately Bradley croaked out, "That's what I'm saying. We can't do it here, Mary, call it off."

But again ignoring him, she looked over her shoulder for the motorcycle. "Drop your window," she said as it pulled up beside them. Then she held her hand out flat toward Bobbie Lee and commanded, "Wait, follow us!"

Now the woman and children were out of the minivan and beginning to move toward the restrooms. The targets' minivan began to back from its spot, then was out. But Coldgrave had already turned and now gave a sharp hand signal to Bobbie Lee to go. Instantly the motorcycle lunged forward and then slid to a stop just at the corner of the targets' front bumper. Bradley quickly pulled up to block the minivan from behind.

The driver lowered his window and stuck his head out, but Connors and Bobbie Lee were off the bike and stepping toward him as he did so. Coldgrave and Packard, now out of the SUV, also approached rapidly. All kept to the driver's side.

"J'ou haf blocked my way," he said with annoyance to Connors, who was now at his window.

She answered him by pulling her gun from her jacket pocket and firing point-blank into his forehead—*Whap!* But even as his head was knocked backward by the blast and his body went limp the four began firing into the vehicle, blowing the windows in and shooting into the bodies of the men with fierce rapidity. Bobbie Lee fired in through the windshield at the front passenger, while Coldgrave and Packard fired in through the side and rear side windows at the three in the back. Glass fragments, nearly aerated by the barrage, seemed still to be settling as the firing ceased.

Nearby the woman, who had let out a horrific scream at the gunfire, fell down upon the sidewalk, and frantically began pulling the children down with her. But before they had settled, the thing was done. Emitting bird-like screeches, she watched in horror as the macabre scene was protracted when Connors and Bobbie Lee reloaded and methodically shot into the heads of the men to make sure they were dead. All around the scene bystanders, some who had been entering or exiting their cars or the restrooms, some who had been simply engaged in idle talk, now stood silently watching as the grotesque drama closed. Then most began to move back or away, a few began to run, some just got into their cars or went back into the restrooms.

With a casual air, Coldgrave stuck her head halfway in through the driver's window and looked at the five men. Oddly the scene, with its five shot-up corpses covered with pieces of glass and flesh, seemed rather compact, even organized, as if nature had arranged it personally. When she had seen enough, she stepped back from the window. For a moment she let her gaze go to the few remaining onlookers. Then she turned and nonchalantly strode back toward the SUV. "All right, good job," she said, "time to go, everyone."

As Bobbie Lee goosed the Harley Connors took a casual look at the sky, the trees, the cars, even the staring people, all as if she had indeed been refreshed by the road stop. Leisurely she pulled her gloves and helmet on, popped the chinstrap home, then swung onto the bike. Bobbie Lee then throttled up and, with a blatting roar from the motorcycle's exhaust, sent them toward the exit. The SUV followed, and soon both vehicles had exited the grim scene.

Once the two vehicles were on the open road and had separated, Coldgrave opened her phone and executed the speed dial. "Bob? . . . Yes, it's done. Everything went well, we're heading home now. . . . No, no one hurt. . . . What am I supposed to say to that, Bob? I have no idea what you'll hear about it. . . . Well, I don't like repeating myself, but again, it went well. . . . Right. . . . Talk to you later."

Bradley shot her a glance. "Did he give you a hard time?"

With a sigh, "Not really. He just said he wondered what kind of a mess he'd hear about this time."

"You should have told him," growled Packard, "to stick that kind of comment."

"I can't believe he really used the word *mess*," said Bradley. "They don't want us using poisons or explosives, yet they want bodies with no leakage. Weird."

Gretchin touched the back of Coldgrave's seat. "Mary, I think you've got glass in your hair, you should brush it out."

Pulling her visor down and taking a look, "Oh—yes, I will."

"It's on the top and a little at the back. If you turn a little, I'll take a look. You don't want it falling into your eyes."

When Coldgrave had turned, Gretchen brushed the glass bits off lightly with her fingers. As she did so she looked for just a moment into the beautiful face, with its reddened lips, its wayward eye, but long enough to see the woman behind the beauty. For the first time, she felt she could excuse Bradley's stolen glimpses. No, she could not blame him or anyone for looking at this woman or indeed for wishing to see more of her. For there was a power in her, a sensuous, even sensual power, a force that could quite easily both capture and slay.

"There," she said, finishing, "you're fine. You might want to keep your eyes closed in the shower though."

"Thank you, Gretchin," replied Coldgrave. Then with a sigh, "Is anyone thirsty? I'm getting a little parched. Perhaps we could pull in somewhere for refreshments, what do you think?"

Bradley shrugged. "I could go for a hamburger, I guess. A hamburger is healthy, it's a complete meal. . . . No beer, though, since I'm driving."

"Oh, don't worry," said Coldgrave cheerily, "if you go tipsy on us, Bradley, I'll drive."

Packard, who had been fiddling with his coat, suddenly uttered, "Ah dammit, there's a hole in my pocket. I'm sure I brought six speed loaders with me. I guess I lost one at the site. Oh what the hell, some kid'll find it and get himself a handful of free bullets."

CHAPTER 15

It was one week later that Willard and a new driver arrived at the Estate for a visit. The agent's face seemed like that of a child as Maggie presented him with a cup of tea and a little plate of chocolate chip cookies. She did not miss the hunger on his face as he crammed two of his four cookies into his mouth, then slurped and burbled at his tea. Neither did she miss the anxiety that had been on Willard's face since he arrived.

"You realize, don't you," he said to them all, after the usual introduction from Coldgrave, "that you gunned down these men right in front of children? Their mother said in her report that she was frightened out of her mind and that her children all cried for the rest of the day and experienced serious nightmares throughout the night. There were literally hundreds of people around. It was a rest stop, for goodness' sake, with public restrooms for travelers." Here he held his hands out, as if to plead with them. "You ruined everyone's Thanksgiving, can't you see that? Again, Mary, I have to put it to you first as team leader, was there no alternative?"

Lowering her glass and giving it a swirl to slosh the gin over the ice, "I thought it appeared to be somewhat crowded, and Bradley said it was far too crowded. But then I decided just to go for it, and there you have it."

His eyes went shut for a moment. "I know, I know, you're going to say it was a success, but I'm telling you no, it wasn't a success, Mary. The Agency doesn't see it that way at all. I couldn't believe the reports from the cleanup crew and from the public. The crew described the site as horrific, like a Bonnie and Clyde thing. And many of the public, those from New Jersey, I suppose, said they were sure it was a Mafia hit job. The Agency expects you to conduct yourselves professionally. I've stressed this so many times now—how many times do I have to say it?"

"I think," she replied, "at least I concluded at the time, that it was all carried out efficiently."

"You know," he continued, as if she had not spoken, "these men were simply diplomats, not out and out criminals to be gunned down, slaughtered like so much scum."

Bradley, his chin dropping nearly to his chest, put in, "That actually has bothered me quite a lot, Bob. I hope your people at the Agency gave this a lot of thought before you sent us out. These were essentially innocent people we killed. I mean, I personally didn't actually shoot anybody, I stayed in the car. Neither did Gretchin, she stayed with me, but the rest did."

Gretchin's eyes widened with fury. "I cannot believe you just said that, Bradley, you stupid fucking asshole!"

Here the driver stopped inserting his now fourth set of two cookies and stared at her in disbelief. Willard himself looked to Bradley for help, but encountering only a sheepish grin, dropped his gaze and looked around at the team's shoes. There was an utter silence as she stood.

"You know, Bradley," she said, "I seriously doubt you've got a morsel of integrity in your whole goddamn body. You drove the car, Bradley, you killed those men as surely as anybody did. I did, too, I manned the phone. Don't you open your eyes when you watch movies, you goddamn fucking moron?"

He looked up at her, for he had avoided her eyes as she spoke. "Well, mainly," he replied meekly, "I wanted to say I was bothered that they were just diplomats. Didn't it bother you too?"

"No, it didn't bother me," she yelled back at him. "We never know the actual guilt or innocence of anybody on any of the projects. Where have you been exactly, out to lunch?"

With both hands he brought his foot up to his knee. "Well, that's where we differ, Gretchin. I trust the Agency, and when the Agency says they're guilty, they're guilty, that's all there is to it. But here it was just revenge, and against people who according to the Agency hadn't done anything. And that bothers me. Let's put it this way—I'm glad I just drove the car."

She sat down again. "For me," she said, pointing to herself with both hands, "for myself, I don't care if they were guilty or innocent, because I'm looking at the bigger picture. I know that's hard for you to get your head around, Bradley, mental invalid that you are, but it's true." And with that she took her eyes off him and sat breathing hard.

"I thought," he said, his voice growing even meeker, "that you were concerned only for your own yard. How is your yard the bigger picture?"

Controlling herself, "I mean that I'm concerned for the global picture as it relates to me, just to me. Forget it, you'll never get it, Bradley."

Willard cleared his throat, then said cautiously, "Getting back to the operation, uh, the project, I'm here to express the concerns of the Agency. And frankly, they're concerned about conduct and appearance. Sure they care about results, but not at any cost. This conversation I'm having with you—the team as a unit—is getting to be a regular thing. It's disturbing, that's all. I wish I knew how to fix it."

"How about failure?" offered Packard.

Willard looked at him. "What?"

"I said failure. You can fix it by having us fail."

"And how would that be a fix, Leonard, may I ask?"

The grayed man folded his arms. "If we fail, you can say Kessler was wrong, and that minimally trained agents are not as effective as fully and properly trained agents. Then you can send us to your schools and turn us into politically correct bastards who aim to make a difference. In short, you need to have us fail so you can justify training us to do things the right way."

Wryly, "I know what you're saying, Leonard. We've weighed the pros and cons of this kind of team quite thoroughly, I can assure you. And you're right, so far, the pros outweigh the cons, which is the only reason the team is still in operation. We know all that."

Coldgrave looked askance at him. "Then what is the essence of the message you brought to us today, Bob?"

He looked down for a moment, then answered, "Very simply, the same as it was the last time— when you execute a project, try to be a little less brutal and a little less obvious."

"Meaning, less public."

"Exactly."

"Because," she added, looking at her gin as she gave it another swirl over its ice, "you don't really care about the brutality, do you? I mean, the Agency doesn't care, do they?"

Momentarily and with a sigh. "No, they don't, they don't seem to."

Bobbie Lee, ready to pop a cookie into her mouth, put in, "We did leave that minivan a little air conditioned and those guys a little shot up. I punched a lot of holes in them heads mysilf. But so what if it was a mess, that's what cleanup crews are for, cleanin' up messes, right?" And when he did not answer, "So, I hope they pay you real good for making these trips out to see us." And then putting the cookie into her mouth and talking around it, "But then, it's always good to see you, Bob, sort of."

His face reddening, he turned to give the agent a see-what-I-mean look, then reached for his tea.

Maggie, who had been watching the level in Coldgrave's glass, stood, took it and left for the kitchen. No one spoke until she had returned with the freshened drink. Coldgrave then took it and straightway drank half of it, as if to complete the theater.

"So," said Connors to Willard, "yous don't want keds to see the kellin's, loike?"

He let his gaze drift over the blond hair and into the colorless eyes. "No, we don't, as I've said before. We would like you to try to avoid that kind of thing, if you can." And when not a muscle in her face moved, he added, "Is that workable for you?"

"Sher."

And just what, he wondered, did that mean? The look in her eyes was saying to him exactly what it had always said, that she was an autonomous entity in the universe and that she would very simply kill anyone who threatened that absolute independence. Considering that the mind behind those eyes was demonstrably incapable of fear, yet very capable of turning living organisms into dead ones, he felt forced to swallow hard before replying, "Fine."

Bradley held up a forefinger. "But I've said that all along. In many ways, we should be following the same rules as everybody else."

Willard looked at him. Here it was, the voice of the only sane member of the team, the one voice in fact that could be counted on to truly serve posterity. "Thank you, Bradley," he replied with obvious gratitude, "I appreciate your sensitivity. The way I see it, sensitivity is the one characteristic that distinguishes the man from the dog."

From a darkened corner, where she had been sleeping, the German Shepherd Helga suddenly roused herself and emitted a low, yet distinctly malignant growl.

"I think," offered Gretchin, "the dog is saying the man is full of shit."

He looked at her. If in Bradley there was sanity, in Gretchin, as in all the others, there was nothing but a kind of impudent insanity. Why was it that every encounter with these people made him think how life would have gone better for him had he simply chosen another profession? He was never mistreated by either his father or his mother. He had never failed in school or in church. He was not given to abuse or addiction. In fact, nothing in his life ever could be blamed for bringing him to this crucible, except his initial choice of profession. He had stepped from a cliff upon that decision. Dealing with people like these not only could but would eventually ruin a man. After looking from Bradley to Gretchin to Helga, he ventured yet another inquisitive look into the strange eyes of Connors. He had not in fact become a saintly public servant, but a manager, a kind of keeper of weird, dangerous, nearly psychotic people.

Coldgrave drained the glass. "Bob, is there any information about another project, or of one in the making? This last one was charming."

He felt his throat tighten at this description. In some ways, this one was the weirdest of the bunch. And just how in the name of grace should he answer her but with the truth, that he indeed had brought information on a new project. *Charming*, really? The images provided to him by the cleanup crew were still nightmarishly at the front of his mind. The five slain men, bullet holes in their heads, eyes shot out, like five gunny sacks of fresh beets, oozing blood. One of them had half his head gone—the work, no doubt, of Packard's magnum. And the car, with its windshield and windows blown in, blood splattered throughout its interior. He took a deep breath. "Actually," he replied, "you've anticipated me, Mary, I do have a new project for the team, yes."

"Oh, good," she returned, "just let me take a little break here, and then we'll all listen as you tell us about it."

He watched as she got up to leave, obviously to use the bathroom. If his intake of liquid was as much as hers, he would be needing a bathroom, too. She had taken the empty glass with her and would doubtless refill it before returning. A few minutes later, glass in hand, she came back, took her seat, crossed her legs, and with freshly painted lips smiled at him pleasantly, as if to say that obviously now she was ready to listen to his little presentation.

CHAPTER 16

"Uh, okay," he said, forcing himself to look away from her, "let's take a look at the new project." He blinked a few times as he looked at them, then brought his hands together and blinked again, as if waiting for them to quiet down.

But as they were already quiet, his antics were not lost upon them, especially not upon Gretchin, who said, her tone rife with disdain, "Don't worry about us, Willy, we love to hear bullshit."

He forced himself to look at her, for he loathed her. Never in his life had he encountered such an insolent person. And how, in goodness' name, had she discovered the nickname he most dispised in all the world—Willy? Leave it to her, leave it to the devil. He swallowed, knowing that if now he complained, she would never let the nickname go. Finally he smiled. "I suppose, Gretchin, you have something on your mind, something you want to discuss?"

"No, no," she returned innocently, "I'm perfectly content, just go on with your story. We're listening, like children, to every word you say."

Jiminy Christmas, he exploded inside, which was as close as he could come to swearing, how he hated this woman! For a brief moment he imagined ordering the driver to simply take her outside and shoot her.

"Really," she added, sensing his anguish, "just go on, Bob, we're listening. Hurry, or you'll lose the opportunity for making a powerful opening statement to the class. By the way, I already have a gold star—that fucking Paul Kessler used to give them out, you know. He saw us as children, too. Yeah, great guy, just like you."

And as he gulped at this, Coldgrave put in, "Yes, Bob, please, go on."

A snicker came from Bobbie Lee. "Yeah, we're a-waitin'. Let 'er rip, Bob."

He cleared his throat, put his hands together again, then quickly separated them and lifted his chin. "Anyway, you have all heard . . . uh, *we* have all heard of the illegal poaching and trafficking of animals, especially of endangered species. Unfortunately this is an ever-increasing criminal game, which isn't surprising, since the penalties are relatively insignificant and the payoffs are huge. Normally the Agency doesn't get involved, but recently a poaching group based here in the U.S. has ventured into the purchase of explosives and small arms. Also they've generated, so to speak, a number of human corpses. We've decided to put them out of business. . . . How does the project sound to everyone?"

Maggie leaned forward. "Not that it matters, of course, but which animals do these people deal in?"

"Actually they've made a shift from rhinoceros horns to live chimpanzees. Their poachers killed two rangers last year, so we have assumed their business change is because of that. In any case, their poachers have to kill between ten and fifteen chimp family members in order to successfully abduct one baby. It's a brutal business, to say the least, and again, one that doesn't normally concern the Agency. But in this case the interests of the business have possibly moved toward terrorism. So, three people will be your targets, two men and a woman. They work apparently mostly from computers, making an occasional trip to Japan or China. The market is, well, burgeoning in the Asian world."

"Where are these people?" queried Gretchin. "Oh, and are they armed?"

He could not help hesitating, for surely she would use any response he made as a springboard to make some acidic comment. Bolstering himself, he replied, "They're based here, just this side of Pittsburgh, in a quiet rural area, at a kind of ranch on a few acres of land. Intel says they're heavily armed."

"You said they've purchased explosives. So, they're really, really dangerous people?"

Again he hesitated. He wanted to say, *Oh, they're dangerous, but not like you, lady*. But he nodded and answered, "They have purchased explosives, yes, and it's possible they could use them as personal weapons. But the rangers were killed with small arms. In any case, they have AR's as personal weapons, and they've probably been modified for auto. And they have a slew of handguns. Nobody's been in the military or jail. It's a loose operation and they're kind of crazy people, so they've been easy to track. They're all loose cannons, including the girl."

Bradley took his eyes off Coldgrave's legs. "Girl? I thought you said woman, Bob. How old are these people?"

"Good point, Bradley. The guys are in their thirties, the girl is fifteen."

"A mature fifteen?" asked Gretchin.

"Well," he sighed, "sort of. Kind of mature and immature at the same time. According to the intel psychologist, even if the girl acts like a kid, she should be treated as an extremely dangerous adult. She's potentially the group's most dangerous element. We believe she's killed at least two people. She's a bit nuts, kind of a Billy the Kid, if you know what I mean."

Bobbie Lee snickered. "Jist hope we don't hear a '*Hello, Bob*' from her."

He threw her a glance of incomprehension.

"Pictures?" queried Gretchin.

"A few, yes. Only one of the girl. The property is rather pathetic, littered with corrugated metal shacks."

"Probably," she said, "we're going to find some of the animals there."

With a nod, "We've called Best Friends. They'll collect them, whatever condition they're in, and transport them to their facility. But of course, we don't care about any evidence whatever, so just ignore it. As usual, the cleanup guys will take care of everything, including calling in the ATF, if necessary, and the animal care people. Just do your job and walk away. . . . These people practice with their weapons, we know that. You might have your hands full. And whatever you do, don't fail to take the girl seriously."

Packard cleared his throat. "You're putting us up out there at a nice hotel, I guess?"

"Everybody's got a joke today."

With a scratch to his stubble whiskers, "I wasn't joking, sport. It may take a couple of days."

"In that case, Leonard, reasonable accommodations will be in order, of course." But immediately he knew he had said the wrong thing.

"Yeah," said Gretchin, "with pit toilets, a bucket of cold water, and a bar of gritty soap."

Considering that his best response to this was to ignore it, he reached into his satchel, withdrew a manila folder, and began unwinding its string. He stopped, however, and simply handed the whole thing to Coldgrave. "Take a look at that, Mary, when you get a chance. Let me know about any concerns."

Then he stood and motioned for the driver to get up. Awkwardly he shoved his hands into his pockets, impatiently waiting until the other had roused himself from the comfortable couch. Maggie also got up and left to get their coats.

"Had enough of us?" queried Gretchin.

Right on the mark, lady, he wanted to reply. Avoiding her eyes, he said to them all, "Thank you all again so much for the hospitality. And, Maggie, everything, as usual, was delicious."

"Well, thank you, Bob," she returned, handing them their coats, "we've enjoyed having you both. It's been charming."

There was that word again. He did not respond, but simply smiled, and casting a cautious glance toward the dogs in their corner, he turned and, with the driver at his heels, headed for the front door.

CHAPTER 17

"I never realized," he said as they rolled through the Estate's gateway, then turned onto the highway, "how much I was missing before I was married, before Sandy."

"How's that, sir?"

He looked out his window toward the dark trees, which like faceless people seemed to be flying past him, as if deliberately rushing in the opposite direction toward a known end. "You know," he answered. "I guess I mean just being able to go home to a decent, normal human being."

Checking the speedometer, "Yeah, they're pretty strange, sir. Everybody on the team, as far as I could see today, was, well, let's just say I can appreciate that you've got your hands full."

"Think so?"

"You showed more restraint than I would have. Talk about insolence, whew!"

"You mean from Gretchin?"

"Yes, sir. I think I would have punched her about the second time she opened her mouth."

"I suppose I might just lose it, hit her myself sometime. That would be nice, and ha, might keep me from getting an ulcer, right?"

"What would her husband do?"

With a shrug and a wayward look toward the fields, "Oh, probably help me, I guess. The real question is what would *she* do."

"She didn't look too tough, to me, sir. . . . What would she do, do you think?"

A long sigh. "Pull out her gun and kill me on the spot."

"Seriously?"

"Uh-huh."

"But that would be signing her death warrant."

"Uh-huh."

With a chuckle, "Ah, come on, sir, seriously? I don't think so. I think she's just a lot of talk."

"They all say that, the drivers, I mean. You're new. I appreciate your driving me, but you're new. These people are crazy, all of them. Did you hear it when Coldgrave described the project as charming? You should see the pictures I saw of those five men. The cleanup crew said their minivan leaked blood down the sewer when they pulled it up onto the flatbed."

"I know they're serious, sir, I didn't mean that. But people like that Gretchin, well, they've gotta talk the talk, and sometimes they talk it a little too much, you know?"

With another look toward the fields, "I think it's genetic."

"Sir?"

"Like Coldgrave's drinking."

"Hey, what a boozer, sir. I've never seen anybody drink like that."

"No, I mean what they've got—you know, the thing, that thing, that characteristic they've got, and they've all got it, that's for sure. I think it's genetic, that's the best conclusion I can come up with."

"But they're useful, right? The Agency actually recruited them, right?"

"Yes, on both counts."

"They're actually in the Agency, right? They're actually CIA?"

Willard paused, then answered, "Even the Mafia uses thugs that aren't really Mafia. . . . I don't really consider the people on this team to actually be CIA. You're CIA, I'm CIA. We're decent people, we believe in our country, and we want to make a moral difference in the world, that's obvious, I think. But these people, except for Bradley, of course—well, they're slimy, they're creatures of the slime, people you just don't want to have in a world with a Judeo-Christian ethic, if I can put it that way. Do you know what I mean?"

Hesitantly, "I think so."

"I've tried to help them, I really have. But they've resisted me, they've all resisted me, except for Bradley. It's funny, but they see themselves as completely autonomous, they all do, you can tell. Each of them has a psyche that's totally beyond scrutiny. And in this work, that's not only weird but dangerous."

"Yeah, I get it, sir. And you really seem unhappy about it all. Could I ask, why not just use regularly trained agents?"

"I've been saying that. But the Agency wants it this way. They like results, sometimes at any cost, despite what I told the team today. And they're tired of spending money training people to do this stuff, only to have them crack up later. Which is what I was saying, it's genetic, you can't train for it. It's like a gift. And the people on this team have been gifted."

"But would you really put it that way, a gift?"

With a shrug, "Why not? A gift from nature, how's that? I can't account for it, that's for sure. It's not just being able to accurately shoot somebody, you know. It's being able to kill somebody in cold blood, face to face, and stop off for a hamburger on the way home, and maybe have it cooked rare. And even then, to be able to do such a thing repeatedly, as if your psyche was refreshed every time you did it."

"Except for Bradley, you said. And he did seem to be a little different from the rest."

"Correct. Yes, I read him as being more like us. . . . Listen, thanks for hearing me, okay? I don't want to talk about it anymore for now. For as long as I've known them, I haven't been able to deal with it fully, and sometimes, if I think about it too much, it gets the better of me, if I can put it that way. . . . How can nature produce such people?"

"They're right out of folklore, kind of, aren't they?"

He looked again to the gloomy landscape. "Yeah, you're right, I guess they are."

Bradley pulled the blanket up to his chin as he listened for the flush of the toilet. It was funny to be curious about such things. Why was it that life so often placed you in a situation where you couldn't help being curious about something you weren't supposed to know about?

"Hey," said Gretchin, switching off the bathroom light, "you're sure in a hurry. What's the matter, got the hurts for a woman?"

For a moment he watched as she got into her flannels for bed. She was certainly still pleasant to look at, although he would prefer she dyed her hair, since red and gray just didn't seem to go. Following her curves as she tossed her bra aside and pulled the nightgown on, he said, "I suppose I'm just appreciating you, if that's okay."

She switched off the main lamp, "Sure it's okay."

"Do you really like it when men look at you?"

She slipped in beside him and pulled the blankets up. "Of course I do, just like you enjoy looking at women."

"What do you think I'm thinking when I look at them?"

"Who gives a shit, pop, just keep looking. I'll worry when you stop."

How could he tell her that he knew she was being untruthful, that she did, in fact, worry when he looked at women? How could he tell her that he felt her eyes burning a hole through him whenever he looked at Mary? Rolling onto his side, he slipped his arm across her belly and put his nose to her neck. He was glad she always smelled so good.

"What do you think," he murmured, closing his eyes, "are we in for the long haul, or is this a fling?"

She chuckled. It was nice to have him try to be funny. "My assessment," she answered, "is that you're a find-them, feel-them, fuck-them, and forget-them kind of guy, so it's probably a fling."

"Hey, come on, don't be crude, you know what I mean."

"You're not joking?"

"No."

"Well," she said, "we are married, so I suppose we're both here for the haul, as you say. But then, we're not young anymore, which means the haul might not actually be a long one."

"That's gloomy."

"Gloom is something smart people think about, Bradley."

"Meaning?"

With a sigh, "Skip it."

"You always say that."

Another sigh. "Yeah, don't say *gloomy*, just say *negative* or something like that. Next you'll be writing poetry."

"Yeah. And so, what if I did?"

"I'd laugh."

"You always laugh at me."

"You're goddamn right I do."

"Why?"

"It's part of who I am, Bradley, don't worry about it. Don't mind me, I'm a little out of sorts tonight."

In the darkness, his face still against her neck, he rolled his eyes, but then kissed her sweet skin and moved his hand down into her flannel panties. "You smell so good," he murmured.

"Think so?"

"Uhmm."

New York State

As Coldgrave steered the Bentley through the gateway she let her eyes run over the bleak gardens. Still, from her youth, simply coming onto the grounds had brought her peace. There were the great glass greenhouses where the roses were grown. Next to the greenhouses were the selection galleries where the best plants were chosen for entry into the shows. Slowing the Continental, she recalled how each season Dad would stand and then pace and then stand again before the plants until he made his choices for the shows. Mother would be there, too, chirping about this and that, trying not to influence him but nonetheless pushing him to make the decisions he found so difficult. Just beyond the greenhouses was the little grave where the gardeners had buried Bopo, and beyond the grave was the great pool where she had spent so many summer afternoons and evenings swimming with him.

But she must be on, for the party was set for eight. When her phone chirped, she pulled over onto the grass and extracted it from her purse.

"Hi, Bob. . . . Fine, thank you. What's going on? . . . I'm at home now, just arrived. . . . No, Mother and Dad's, I'm here for a party. . . . Actually now's a good time. What's up?" As she listened to the lengthy explanation she lifted the glass from its holder, put it under her nose, and breathed in the alcohol. "Of course we will, Bob, but it is the holiday and I promised to attend the family party. . . . Christmas, I'm sure—I can't think of any other holiday it might be. It is Christmastime, isn't it? . . . Well then, there you are, I was right. Anyway, you'll have to give us a couple of days to prepare, that's all. Then I think we can get out there. . . . Yes, a couple of days. I'll call Maggie now. . . . All right, thanks for calling. We'll get things moving. I'll let you know when we're on the, um, highway. . . . Yes, Merry Christmas to you too and of course to Sandy. . . . All right, bye."

CHAPTER 18

Pittsburgh, December

"This is great," said Gretchin sardonically, unzipping her suitcase, "this is the *what* Inn? Here we are, near a major city, and we can't even get a Marriott. Look at this place. God, the Agency's cheap."

Bradley drew a fresh T-shirt from the bag. "It probably has something to do with security, instead of cheapness. Cut them some slack."

"How about that," she continued, coming from the bathroom, "there's toilet paper, genuine toilet paper. Now I'm happy, now I know somebody at the Agency fucking loves me." She gave him a hard look. "Security, you think it has to do with security?"

"Maybe."

"Len has to double with the girls. What is that? He doesn't need that, and I'm sure Maggie wasn't happy to hear about it. And I don't see how Mary can even stay in a goddamn hole like this. She's used to New York City, posh New York." And holding forefinger and thumb so that they almost touched, "I'm about that close to calling Bob and telling him what I think of him."

"Nothing you would say would come as a surprise, I'm sure."

Ignoring this, "So, is where we are considered rural?"

"Just about, I think. I still think it all has to do with security. And Mary's just down the hall. She's fine, I'll bet."

She looked at him. "Kind of sweet on her, aren't you?"

He did not look at her. "No, but she saved my life, and I think I should meet her where she's at in life."

She threw him a fresh pair of socks from the suitcase. "That sounds a little personal. Maybe where she's at in life isn't your business."

"You said you wanted me to be more sensitive. Now you're making fun of me for trying to do just that. I can't win, can I?"

Her tone went cold. "Not with me, prick, not with me. But you are sweet on her, aren't you?"

"I'm just curious about her *whatever* issues."

"Yeah," she returned, "and that's why you look at her legs, because you're curious about her issues. Sure, I've got it, bub. Look, I know what brings that crank of yours up, and it ain't issues."

Tossing the socks onto the bed, he went into the bathroom and closed the door. For a few moments he heard nothing, but was sure she had approached. Stealthily he reached over and slid home the bolt of the little lock. Then her voice boomed through the door.

"I only hope we get a bigger budget out of Trump than we've gotten out of Obama. I don't want to stay in any more goddamn seedy places, hear me?"

"Yeah, I—I agree," he said so she could hear. Then he heard her phone chime and her talking in a low voice. He flushed the toilet and opened the door.

"All right," she said immediately, her voice like flint, "we're all leaving for dinner in ten minutes. Mary says there's a diner of some sort about a mile away. Hurry up, I'm hungry." But then, giving him a look, "Did you wash your hands?"

Meekly he returned to the bathroom and washed his hands. Then he pulled the T-shirt on, followed by a mock turtle, then a sweater. From the bathroom he heard the voice again.

"Next time you're in here, Bradley, don't splash so much water around."

He wanted to tell her to get herself back to hell, but instead replied with a simple okay and reached for his coat. Somehow since their marriage the impetus for answering her back had diminished. Before, he had answered her in like coin and at times, at least in his estimation, had gotten the better of her. He had even schemed against her, preparing answers to face down her vitriolic criticisms. But since their marriage, since the very day of the wedding, the drive to contend with her had waned significantly.

Later, after he had driven them to the diner and remarked that the food must be fresh since there were so many cars in the parking lot, and she had not responded, he found himself hoping for a malice-free dinner and evening. But after Bobbie Lee and Connors arrived and they had all been seated, he caught her eyeing him, as if preparing to put him in his place.

"This doesn't seem so bad." he ventured, tapping the tablecloth. "The place is practically full. Bet the beer's fresh here." Then he caught her eye, and sensing she was about to pounce, ceased the tapping. Life just wasn't fun anymore, he lamented. It used to be fun driving her nuts by drumming his fingers or whistling or by doing any of the things he had noticed irritated her. Now everything seemed to irritate her and teasing her was no fun at all.

"Are you going to do that anymore?" she queried.

"What?"

"Tap the table. You're not in high school, and you don't have ADD."

"High school?" he came back. "What does tapping the table have to do with high school, dear?"

With a fiery look, "Don't call me that."

He shrugged, then on impulse said, "Let's ask somebody else. Len, do you think tapping the table makes me seem like a high school student?"

Packard looked above his menu. "Maybe just a little, pal."

Catching her smile at this, Bradley picked up his menu. "I'm getting a steak tonight," he announced. "Steak and beer, that's what I want. Everybody else set? Here comes the waitress."

"Server," corrected Gretchin without looking up, "just say server, Bradley, waitress is a pejorative now."

He looked down, then lifted his chin and said to her, "I'll bet you can't spell that."

Before Bobbie Lee switched off the bathroom light, she could hear Packard snoring. Moving past his bed, she turned the thermostat down, then climbed in beside Connors.

"I'm freezin'," she whispered, slipping an arm over Connors middle, "you gotta warm me up, girl."

Connors moved her back closer, hugging Bobbie Lee's arm. "What do you t'ink of t'is kellin' business? Maybe we should, loike, retoire."

With a chuckle, "Sure, girl, that'll be the day. What makes you say somethin' foolish like that? You've got a good million trigger pulls left in you."

Giving the arm another squeeze, "Not sher. Guess I'm feelin' me age."

"Lordy, you're only forty-three, give me a break."

"I've got, loike, about twenty bullet holes en me, so's I can't even walk a straight loine anymore. Maybe et's toime to quet."

"And do what, take up sewin'? I can see you behind a sewin' machine like I can see Mary at an AA meeting. Besides, I think your walk looks pritty straight. As much as I watch your ass, I guess I can swear to it. So, git over it, girl, you'll be here till the cows come home."

"T'ink I've got the chip, loike, eh?"

"For killin'? I would think. I look at it like this. For the dear man in the next bed, bless his heart, this work is strictly business. For Mary, it's candy—she's got enough gin, you understand. For Bradley and Gritchin, it's a little different. For Gritchin, well, I'll take her at her word, I guess she's jist protictin' her yard. For Bradley, it seems to be duty and service and all that. For me, I have to say, it's like beer, it's fun. But for you, girl, it seems to be more like air or food. Now, you wouldn't wanna suffocate or starve to death, would you?"

"Sounds loike bullshet, to me."

"Well, I thought it sounded pritty good, and I'm puttin' it in a book someday, you wait."

"Still, we could beat the systam, quet now."

"Homesick for Irelan'?"

"Et's a possibelity."

"Well, if you wanna quit, retire, I say we go back to Tinnessee. I don't think I'd like livin' in Irelan'."

"Sooner or later a bullet has to gat me roight through me fuckin' heart."

Bobbie Lee swallowed, then tightened her hug. "Don't worry, I'll git you buried real nice. I'll make sure you look like a goddamn angel, trust me, girl."

"Loike, I wanna see me ma and the green, green grass."

"It's green here."

"No, et's not."

After a moment, "You're gittin' gloomy again, you'd better stop. . . . I ain't a fool, I know in this business you don't always live long enough to git to pick your hospice. I imagine people like us can die in pritty ugly places. But don't worry, if you've made your peace with God, you'll jist spring up naked out of a cake and step up to the bar. And if you haven't, well, I guess you'll be in shit soup. Anyway, I'm warm now. Good night, girl, tomorrow's a workday." When there was no answer, she withdrew her arm and turned over.

CHAPTER 19

"Boy, that's a dirty pickup truck," said Bradley, completing a second pass of the property. "And look, no trees around the house."

"This isn't a house situation," added Gretchin from the back seat, "this is a compound."

Continuing to accelerate, "You're being negative, please don't."

"You actually have a problem with my telling it the way it is?"

Beside her, Packard grimaced. "You two gonna start? You're gonna make the coffee boil in my stomach."

"Start what, Leonard?" she shot back. "I'm just giving mister asshole, who happens to be driving this vehicle, my analysis of the situation. What's wrong with that, are you going to have a problem with it, too?"

"Gretchin may be correct," put in Coldgrave, pushing up her visor.

Bradley breathed an audible sigh. "Which means what, Mary?"

"Which means they could be anywhere on the property. Chasing them around there could be hazardous."

"There's one house and then mostly shacks, right? And the shacks are probably for the animals."

"Well then," said Gretchin, "how about it, superman, do *you* want to go in there and search them out? You know, with cape and a big S on your chest?"

Giving the wheel a tap, "I told you, don't be negative."

"Realistic."

"Negative," he insisted, his tone becoming heated. "You're always negative, and I don't like it. You're working against us here, Gretchin."

Coldgrave reached for her phone, clicked speed dialing, then said, "Yes, Kelly, listen, Gretchin feels the situation is precarious, and too dangerous for trying to locate the targets. What do you two think? . . . Uh-huh. . . . Uh-huh. . . . Actually I agree with Gretchin. . . . Uh-huh. . . . Okay, I'll call back in a few minutes, we need to discuss it. . . . Right." Then she closed the phone and sat thinking as Bradley continued to drive.

"So?" queried Gretchin.

Bradley gritted his teeth. "Give her a chance, Gretchin. She already said she agreed with you."

"So?"

"So, she's taking your side, so shut up."

"I'm not taking her side," said Coldgrave, "I'm agreeing with her assessment."

"Well, she was just being emotional, and you know it."

"I don't care about her emotional state, her assessment was accurate."

Gretchin made a mocking click with her tongue. "See, dope?" And when he did not respond, she said to Coldgrave, in her most objective tone, "So, what did Kelly say, Mary?"

Taking a deep breath, "Well, since they've brought the camper, they want to try going in on a pretense, just the two of them. We would be down that, um, road as back-up. . . . I suppose I should say street, *road* is a bit rustic, isn't it?"

Bradley squinted. "Is it? What's the difference? Anyway, you mean we would be there as the second wave, not back-up, right?"

"Oh, certainly, Bradley, thank you, I like that. But what's everybody think?"

"If they go in on a pretense," said Packard, "that'll rule out their use of long guns. You can't just walk up to the door with a long gun."

"Right."

"So," said Gretchin, "they're willing to bet all three are in the house."

"I wouldn't say bet, but Kelly said they both thought they were all in the house."

Bradley cocked his head, "That's a little simplistic, don't you think?"

"Oh God, Bradley, simplistic?" returned Gretchin. "You judge something as being simplistic—*you*?"

Now he slapped the wheel. "Stop it, Gretchin, you're not being helpful."

Her voice rose. "Don't tell me to shut up, fool."

Calmly Coldgrave opened the phone again, but before making the call, said, "I don't think we have many choices here."

"Actually," said Packard, "the pretense thing sounds good to me. We can go in when it starts and head around back."

Then she made the call. "Hi, Kelly, listen, go ahead. But we'll give you just a moment or two and then come in ourselves around to the back, engage as we have to, and probably start checking the back buildings. . . . Right, I understand. So, we'll give you a couple of minutes, then we'll come in whether we hear shots or not. . . . Right, but I can't think of anything else right now. . . . Surely. . . . Gretchin will text you when we're in position. . . . Right, but confirm, okay? . . . All right, bye."

"So," said Bradley, "we're going to do it now?"

She dropped the phone into the purse. "Yes, turn us around."

"But, Mary, that's not much planning, and Bob said the girl's a hotshot."

She glanced at him as he looked for a place to turn around. "I know," she replied, "but Kelly's got a good feel for things. Bobbie Lee does, too. And like I said, I can't think of an alternative right now."

"A good feel for things?" he returned, astonished. "Kelly? She's always going in before she's supposed to. And you're saying she has a good feel for things?"

"Well, I didn't mean it that way. I meant she has a good sense of achieving success. Don't forget, she hasn't failed."

"She's been shot lots of times, Mary. You don't consider it a failure to get shot?"

"No."

But Gretchin put in, "Don't argue, Bradley, just turn the car around."

As Bobbie Lee steered the camper past the SUV Connors turned to see Bradley grinning from his window. For just a moment she pictured herself sleeping with the bastard. But instantly she dismissed the images as repulsive. She wouldn't sleep with the man in a thousand years. Why did life seem bent on presenting you with repulsive possibilities, as if it couldn't stand to let the joys of normalcy go unchallenged?

Pulling on an orange hunter's cap, she said to Bobbie Lee, "Joost pull up there." And as the camper came to a halt, "What do you t'ink? Do I look loike a real duck keller, or what?"

The other sniffed, "Sure, why not, who gives a shit? It's just to git us to the door. Give me the other one." And pulling the rearview mirror over to look at herself, "Me an' you are hunters—hard-ass female hunters, obviously. So, lit's git to it, girl. Front door, ask for dirictions to the nearest state park. When do you wanna open up?"

"I'll joost gat a feel for et."

With a roll of her eyes, "Lit's make a plan this time. If we see two of them, we open up, then git inside, what say?"

Connors tugged at her brim. "Suits me. But I say, the girl first, no matter what."

"No, you're right, you're right on the nickel there. We'd best take the intel seriously, shoot that miss McCarty through the heart real fast."

"Who's t'at?"

"Willian Henry McCarty, Jr.—Billy the Kid. You don't know that?"

"As in Bobbie Lee Henry? Maybe yous two are related."

"Hey, girl, don't make a killer out of me. Like Bob says, I'm on the right side, right? . . . My guess is, she'll be slingin' one of the AR's. And she prob'ly won't even answer the door—goddamn sociopath, prob'ly. Fifteen years old, my ass. Hell, I grew up with meaner kids than her. One kid I knew, he carried a .38 at ten years old, and he used it."

"What happaned to hem?"

"When he was twelve, the police shot him dead in his daddy's Cadillac in a runnin' gun battle right outside of Knoxville. Waste of a really good car—totaled it."

Connors looked at her, then pulled out her phone.

Bobbie Lee gave another sniff, then closed both hands on the wheel. "All right, tell me when, girl."

When the call connected, "We're raddy, Gratchin. . . . We're goin' en as hoonters askin' for dirations. Ef we gat two of tham togather, we're openin' foire, loike. . . . Yeah, yous can't come en too soon. . . . I don't care ef yous come en too late, joost not too soon. . . . I don't care how yous do et, take a fuckin' guess. . . . Foine. All roight, tan saconds and we're goin' en."

Watching as the phone was put away, Bobbie Lee began to take deep breaths.

"Okay," said Connors, "do et."

Bobbie Lee accelerated and moments later was steering the camper up the long driveway of ice and dirt. After navigating the rutted drive, she pulled them up before the front porch, left the engine running, and pulled the handbrake.

Leisurely they got out, climbed the two steps, and stepped up to the door.

Raising her eyebrows, Bobbie Lee said, "That's lead paint, look at that." And pressing the button, then giving a knock, "That ain't healthy."

After only seconds, the inside door was opened and a man in a sweatshirt, clearly one of the targets, stepped up to the rusty screen.

"Yes?" he queried amiably, his eyes moving over them and the camper.

"Well, sir," said Bobbie Lee, pushing her cap up, "sorry to bother y'all, but I think we've lost the road. You wouldn't know where the state park is, would you?"

"Which one?"

"The closest one, I guess. We got lost coming out of Pittsburgh."

"Hunters?"

With a grin, "Jist a little." But then she saw the girl and the muzzle of the AR slung on her back as she came into the room behind him.

"Whatcha after?"

Certain that Connors, just to her right, had not yet seen the girl, she slipped her hand into her coat pocket and replied casually, "Why, we're after you, sir."

Deftly she pulled the P-64, took half a step to her left, and fired four times through the screen at the girl—*Bam! Bam! Bam! Bam!* Connors, reading it perfectly, fired her .38 three times into the man's face—*Pop! Pop! Pop!*—knocking him backward.

As Bobbie Lee twisted and pulled on the doorknob to get the screen door open she saw the girl, the rifle still slung over her back, struggle to her hands and knees, then scramble into the room behind. Balling up her fist, Bobbie Lee punched through the rusty screen, felt for the latch and lifted it.

Once inside they rushed into the next room after the girl. Instantly they were met by two huge blasts as the girl fired from where she lay wailing on the floor. Bobbie Lee, hit twice in the leg, simply dropped, but Connors fired two answering shots, hitting the girl in the midsection. Then pulling her Baby Glock from her other pocket, she stepped over to the girl, leveled the muzzle at her temple and fired, blowing the top of the forehead away. As she turned to Bobbie Lee she heard a door slam at the rear of the house and the SUV running by under the windows.

With shouting and gunfire sounding from outside, she turned Bobbie Lee onto her side. "Where?" she demanded.

Grasping at her left knee, Bobbie Lee screamed out angrily, "My lig, my knee. Jesus! Goddamn girl!"

Connors pulled the bloody hand away to have a look. She identified two holes—one in the back of the leg, just above the knee, the other through the thigh. Retrieving the P-64, she laid it beside

Bobbie Lee. "Dedn't het the knee. Joost keep squeezin' t'at lag, both places. Here's your gun. I'll be back."

Bobbie Lee followed Connors with her eyes as she left, then looked over at the girl. The forehead, like a hunk of meat with the corner cut off, oozed blood. Just above the body, the silly, brightly colored characters of a dated cartoon played out their slapstick on an old TV.

Outside, the team had surrounded one of the back buildings, where the target had taken refuge. With Packard covering the rear, and Bradley one of the sides, Coldgrave used the SUV as cover as she listened as the man shouted from behind a plywood door.

"So?" said Connors to her impatiently. "What about t'is fucker, why's he stell aloive, loike?"

Coldgrave presented a smile of frustration, replying, "I'm not sure I know." Then she motioned for Bradley to come over, and then said to him, "Get in the car, get ready to push the building over."

"Whoa," he breathed, "why didn't I think of that? That's just corrugated steel on a wood frame. Sure, that'll work."

"What's he yellin' about in there?" asked Connors. "What's he want?"

Coldgrave looked down. "He says he has two chimps in cages and that he'll kill them and himself if we don't let him go. He says he just wants to get to his truck."

"What's he got?"

"Judging from the two holes in my door over there, I'd say either a .41 or .44 magnum."

Connors wiped her nose with the back of her gun hand. "Bobbie Lee's hurt, two .223's t'rough the lag. Bleedin's not too bad, but we should gat her to a hospetal soon."

"I hope I don't get myself killed here," muttered Bradley as he backed the SUV, then aimed it at the shed. "Stay behind the car." Slowly he brought the bumper up to the plywood door.

"All right," said Coldgrave, "let's give him a chance." Then in a louder voice she spoke to the man inside. "Okay, buddy, you have one chance, right now, and you'll not get a second. Throw the gun out, come out with your hands where we can see them, and we'll put you in your truck. . . . What do you say? You have only a few seconds. Make your choice."

Momentarily the door was cracked, then opened wider. The gun was thrown out onto the SUV's hood. Then a raised hand emerged, then the other, as the man walked out.

"You'd better let me go," he snarled, "I'm trustin' you guys. You'd better let me go, I just want to go, that's all. No trouble, no trouble, just let me go. You can have the chimps, they're worth a lot."

They spread out, their weapons leveled, as he moved around the SUV and toward them, his hands aloft. Packard, lowering his 686, came from the rear and stood to the side.

"Keep the hands up, way up," ordered Coldgrave, with the muzzle of her .38 trained on him. "Walk toward me, and then toward your truck. Keep the hands up."

As Gretchin left to attend to Bobbie Lee, Bradley and Packard watched as Coldgrave marched the man along the side of the house toward the pickup.

"Get in," she ordered.

"My keys are in the house."

"Just get in," she returned. When he had climbed in and sat looking at her through the open door, she said, "All right, that's the deal, you're in your truck." Then she steadied the muzzle and pulled the trigger, shooting him in the head. As he fell across the seat, she casually walked to the other side, pulled open the door, and fired four times, into the top of his head. Not bothering to shut the doors, she returned to the SUV, reloading as she went.

Bobbie Lee, now inside the SUV and still clutching her leg, but more because of the pain than to stem the bleeding, sat uttering curses as Gretchin closed the door. "Goddamn .223's," she yelled, "I hate them things, they sting like a fuckin' wasp."

Suddenly the report of five muffled shots came from inside the house. Moments later Connors leisurely emerged from the back door. "I joost wanted to make sher about the one at the front door," she said as she reloaded.

After taking a look at Bobbie Lee's wounds, Coldgrave told her simply to keep the pressure on. Then she asked Bradley, who had come from the shed, if only the two chimps were inside.

He nodded gravely. "They seem to be in fairly good shape, but they're scared, and they're cold, they're shivering. There's no heat in there."

She took out her phone and opened it. "Hello, Bob, it's done. . . . Correct. . . . Bobbie Lee's taken two .223's to the left leg. Blood's under control for now with just pressure, but she's in quite a bit of pain. . . . No, both went all the way through, exit holes not too bad, but the leg's useless. We're heading out now. We'll be going through Pittsburgh, so text me where you want us to take her. Oh, and there were only two animals, both chimps. They're frightened and quite cold, and they need attention right away. . . . No, that's too long, definitely too long. I told you, they're frightened. . . . Okay, fine. Talk to you later. . . . Uh-huh."

"When?" asked Gretchin.

"Three to four hours, which means longer, of course." Meeting the aqua eyes, she said, "You don't have to say it, Gretchin." And then to Bradley, "Can the cages be moved?"

"Oh sure," he returned, "both cages are small, too small, if you ask me."

Pulling her shooting gloves up tighter, then touching one of the bullet holes in her door, "We can't wait for the crews, you and Kelly take them home in the camper. We'll head for the hospital."

CHAPTER 20

On the day before Christmas Eve, Willard came to meet with the team and discuss the project. Having let his driver go home for the holiday, he arrived instead with Sandy, who sat with him on the couch, perfunctorily cooing over Maggie's special holiday tea and Christmas fruitcake and cookies.

"I have to have the recipe to this fruitcake, Maggie," she said, her eyes sparkling. "Otherwise I will accuse you of hording great art."

Unable to suppress her delight, the other flushed. "I'm glad you like it, Sandy, I'll send the recipe home with you. We're all so glad you've come. More tea?"

But Willard sat uneasy, his eyes upon Bobbie Lee's wrapped leg. He frowned as he looked at her wheelchair and watched her drink her beer and make jokes with Connors. Something within him recoiled from such a display of joy. He wondered how anyone could be so content, so happy after having just had two bullets blow through her leg at three thousand feet per second.

"Bob," said Coldgrave at length, "did you want to start soon?"

"What? Oh yes, sure, sure. Would now be a good time?"

"Certainly. I'll introduce you."

With a confident frown, "That won't be necessary, Mary."

But she turned to the group and said, "If I may have everyone's attention. . . . It's so good of Bob and Sandy to visit us at, um—" Here she stopped and threw an inquisitive look in Maggie's direction.

"At Christmastime," said the other.

"Yes, at Christmastime, of course. Thank you, Maggie, those things slip my mind sometimes."

He watched patiently as she paused the introduction to take a hefty pull at the gin. "Mary," he ventured, "I'm sure I can just—"

Swallowing, she turned to him. "Yes?"

His eyes going closed, "Never mind, please continue."

She raised the glass, took a mere sip, then said, "Yes, well, we're all happy you two can be with us. Now, Bob, I know you want to discuss the project. Why not tell us what's on your mind?"

He looked around at them. Everyone except Bradley seemed to be conveying a kind of unconditional resistance to anything he might have to say. At length he swallowed, then said, "Thank you, Mary, for that introduction. I, *we*, both Sandy and I, are happy to be here with everyone." He paused, straightened his back, then continued. "So here we all are again. I do want to discuss the project. As usual, I represent the Agency, of course, although not everything I say is necessarily from them."

Gretchin reached for a beer. "Bob," she said, "could you just cut the bullshit? What's your problem this time?"

Deep within himself he wished to ignore her. He had done so before, and with some success, treating her as a mere heckler. He flushed, looked around, then said directly to Bobbie Lee, "As an aside, Ms. Henry, should you be drinking—I mean, with all the pain medicine you're taking?"

Bobbie Lee, caught with a mouthful of beer, at first stared at him, then swallowed, and made a piggish sound through her nose. "Hadn't thought of that, Bob," she replied, "guess you're right. Wouldn't want to mix codeine and alcohol— prob'ly fry my goddamn liver." Here she took another swig of beer and looked at him.

"I'm sorry you were hurt," he said, his tone sympathetic. "It must be very painful. You can't use the leg at all, I mean, for now?"

Another swig, then, "Uh-huh."

"Um, you mean—yes to which?"

Giving him a look, "Yeah, it fuckin' hurts, and no, I can't use the lig. That's why I'm sittin' in a wheelchair, Bob."

"One shot tore up the ligaments, and the other just missed the thigh bone?"

"That's what they tell me."

He wanted to tell her a thing or two himself, such as how much the surgery cost. But after a hawkish look from Gretchin, he took a deep breath and said, "Anyway, the project was a success, you just have to look at it that way. I wish you a speedy recovery. You did a fine job."

"How do you know?" she returned, "you weren't there." And to Connors she said, "Did you tell Bob here I did a fine job?"

Connors shook her head.

"Well, there you go, Bob, Killy here didn't tellya and I didn't tellya, and since nobody else was there, how do you know I did a fine job? How do you know I didn't jist fuck it up and git mysilf shot for my trouble?"

He threw her a cold look. "I guess I don't know. But the whole thing turned out okay, it seems to me."

"So your praise, at least to me, is perfunctory."

With an impatient shrug, "I wouldn't say that. Again, the project turned out fine, so I would say everyone did a fine job. That's not perfunctory." He could not help throwing a glance in Gretchin's direction, but kept his chin up. "Besides, I was being positive, which is a good thing, and I don't apologize for it. So, that's it, I think. . . . Now, if I could, I'd like to discuss other things, some not so positive."

Coldgrave looked into her glass, which was empty. "Excuse me for just a moment," she said, "I must refresh my drink." And getting up, "Don't wait for me, Bob, just go right ahead. I'm sure everyone is anxious to hear what you have to say."

But he did wait, they all did, for the refreshment of Coldgrave's drink had become an integral part of life for all of them. When she had returned and taken her place, he looked up at her and watched as she put the glass to her nose and inhaled its vapors. Then, suddenly aware that Sandy was watching him, he straightened his back again, looked around at them all, and spoke.

"I wish I could say that everything about the execution of the project was perfect."

"But," put in Gretchin, "you can't."

He smiled. "But criticism can be helpful, wouldn't you agree, Gretchin? That's what critique is, right?"

"Oh sure," she returned, stuffing a handful of hair behind an ear. "But you're pathological about it, aren't you?"

Without thinking, he shot back, "No more than you are to your husband, I could say."

Her eyes went hot and her tone cold. "Don't you ever try to get into my personal life, prick. And that goes for the Agency too. They may hide their cameras in my toilet, if that's what jerks them off, but if they, or you, ever try to get into my personal life, I'll sure as hell respond."

He stared at her, his chest tightening, then glanced at Sandy. "You know, Gretchin," he offered, "your point would be just as clear if you didn't swear."

She nodded. "You're lecturing me?"

"You could do with a lecture or two."

"And you're preaching to me?"

"You could do with a sermon or two."

"Do you know why they have swear words?"

His tone sardonic, "I'm not sure I do, actually."

"To penetrate the impervious insensitivity of people like you."

"And you're not insensitive?"

"Of course I am, that's why I swear even to myself. Maybe that's what I need to navigate life. Maybe it's the way I touch reality as I try to survive this goddamn world. What's the difference, fucker?"

"So," put in Coldgrave, "what critique of our work did you want to offer, Bob?"

He swallowed, looked again to Sandy, who had dropped her eyes, then back to Coldgrave.

"Yeah," put in Gretchin, her eyes now a sulfuric green, "we gave you three bodies and rescued two animals, what critique would you offer, Bob?"

His chest tightened even more, so that he could barely speak. "Could you just wait, Gretchin, is that possible? I have certain things I would like to discuss, that's all. Just give me the chance, would you, is that possible?"

She leaned back in her chair and waved a hand at him. "Oh sure, take your time, Bob, we're all listening."

He swallowed hard as he became aware that her sudden nonchalance was emphasizing his glowering at her. Then he felt Sandy's hand on his arm and heard Maggie asking if either of them would like more tea.

Sandy smiled, "No, thank you, Maggie. You, Bob?"

His face full of pain, "Uh, no, no, thanks, I'm fine."

Coldgrave lowered her glass. "So, continue, if you would, Bob, we're listening."

Struggling to regain his composure, he moistened his lips several times before speaking. "I have only two things, I guess, to mention. Now, again," here he threw a cautious glance in Gretchin's direction, "not to be overly critical, but the project's execution seemed a little extreme, if I can use that term." Here he looked around for a response, but finding only disinterest, he continued, "The report from the cleanup crew said that the face of the man at the front door looked as if it had been butchered. Was that necessary? And the pickup truck's doors had been left wide open, as if to present the gory scene to the neighbors." Again he looked around at them. Shaking his head, he continued, "It's this kind of brutality—again, if I can use that word—that I'm concerned about. I mentioned it before, but it still seems to be there. The people over me at the Agency have mentioned it to me now a number of times." He followed this last statement with numerous blinks. "What am I to give them as an answer?"

"You could always tell them," offered Gretchin, "to go fuck themselves."

CHAPTER 21

"Nice," he returned. "Thanks so much for that sensitive, intelligent response. But what actually am I to say to them? The other teams don't execute their projects this way, they're all more, what shall I say, more professional about it. And I don't know, even for myself, what the point is exactly when this team executes a project in such a vicious way."

"There's an old saying," replied Packard, giving his grizzled chin a scratch, "shoot 'em in the foot, they limp away, shoot 'em in the ass, they hobble away, shoot 'em in the head, they don't go anywhere. And," holding up his trigger finger, "never kill 'em once, always kill 'em twice."

As Willard looked at him he could not help wondering how such an antiquated perspective had survived the onslaught of modernity. "Well, Leonard, I guess I can understand the logic of that, sure. But you get where I'm coming from too, I hope."

The response was more growl than speech. "I don't want to get where you're coming from, bud. If you don't like my services, fire me."

"Well, let me put it this way. There is huge potential for tension between the necessary actions of the Agency, especially when operating within the United States, and the public, or at least the public's perception. So, a balance of, say, appearance and reality, must be struck. You understand, I'm sure. We all know these things. With this work, well, there's something awful about it. It's part of my job to sort of minimize the awfulness of it, sort of clean it up a bit."

Gretchin gave him a wry smile. "We know all this. But obviously what we're saying is that the successful completion of the job, the absolute destruction of the targets, takes priority over everything else, including our own safety. If the public require propriety and safety so they won't pee their pants, let them watch TV—you know, finger outside the trigger guard, calling 'clear,' like idiots, to let everyone know a room is empty, and all the other fluffy shit that reduces the awfulness of it all. We don't operate that way, and we won't operate that way. And if the Agency or you don't like the way we do things, well, you can fucking fire all of us."

"I understand that, Gretchin, I do."

"Then why the hell do you keep bringing it up?"

He looked at the floor again, then up at her, then at Bobbie Lee. "You mention safety. Look at Ms. Henry there. Don't you think a little more attention to safety would be helpful? Better yet, let me ask Ms. Henry that. Well?"

Bobbie Lee swallowed, then lowered the bottle to rest upon her leg. "That's rhetorical. I hate rhetorical quistions, they're insulting. I turn them into interrogatives. So, then the answer would be no."

Coldgrave cleared her throat. "Wasn't there another thing you wanted to mention, Bob?"

"Actually there was," he replied. "I'm curious as to why we found the third target in the pickup truck. Your report stated that he had been isolated to the shed. How did he get to the truck?"

"I made a deal that if he gave up, we'd put him in his truck."

He gave her a puzzled look. "That's very odd, don't you think? I mean, it seems somewhat sentimental on your part, and dangerous too, I might add."

"I was concerned about the animals, the chimps. He was threatening to kill them, then himself, if we didn't let him go. He said he wished to get to his truck. So, I offered him the deal, he accepted, threw his gun out, and I took him to his truck. There was no problem, it was all quite charming, almost theatrical."

"So, he came out unarmed?"

"Yes."

"You took him to the truck in order to honor your part of the deal? Which was very moral, I admit, but also quite dangerous. He might have turned on you or even escaped entirely. You were concerned about keeping your part of the deal?"

"Oh, no," she answered, as if surprised. "I wasn't thinking of it quite like that, no. I was concerned about the smell of blood."

"The—" he stammered, "the smell of blood?"

"Yes, I was concerned that if I simply shot him there, the smell of his blood would upset the chimps. So, I walked him to his truck, told him to get inside, then shot him. It was all quite—how would you put it, Maggie?"

The other raised her eyebrows. "Oh, you mean, *tidy*?"

"Yes, exactly, that's perfect, tidy, it was all quite tidy."

"So," he said, clearly uninterested in the nicety of this term, "not being a moralist, of course, you had no problem hammering his head with bullets, while taking care not to, even possibly, disturb the chimpanzees with the smell of his blood."

"Correct," she answered. And raising the glass to her lips, she looked over its rim at Gretchin, then Maggie.

He put his hands together and looked at her for a moment, as if to consider the oddity of it all. "Let me ask you something, Mary. Which would you say is more valuable, a man or a chimp?"

"It would depend upon the situation."

"Would it?"

"Certainly."

"Well, how about a dog, then?"

"Same thing."

After a moment, "So, within the scope of this project, you would say that the chimps were more valuable than the man?"

"Yes."

Now his look became a stare.

Then Gretchin said, "I agree with Mary."

He looked at them all, then said to Coldgrave, "Do you think, Mary, that's a moral perspective?" And when she merely looked at him for this, he said, "I assume that when you say you're not a moralist, what you really mean is that you don't want someone else or even society to determine your morality. Is that right?"

After taking a brief moment to consider the amount of gin left in the glass, she answered, "That's probably fair to say. I think I'm what I want to be and how I want to be. This is who I am and how I want to be. If I want to view a person or situation primarily from a moral perspective, or not, I will do so."

"Forgive me, I know you people say you're not overtly religious, but where does it leave God, to say ever that an animal is of more value than a human being?"

"I would say," she answered, giving the gin a slosh over the ice, "that it leaves God alone—in the sense that it refrains from meddling with what is his business. Someone more religious than I, which perhaps means you, might feel free to so meddle. I would not. I would also say that all creatures have value before God. But this project was not about religion, it was about society, and as to society, this man and the others had forfeited their value, and the chimpanzees had not."

He considered this for a moment, then said, "Do you agree with that, Leonard?"

There was a gleam in the wolfish eyes as the grayed old killer responded. "Sure," he answered, exposing yellow teeth. "I'd even say more than that. I'd say that the man was of negative value to society and needed to have his goddamn head blown off. I'm not some militant animal lover or anything like that, but yeah, I'd say the man needed to be destroyed and the chimps needed to be rescued."

"I guess I don't need to point out," said Willard at length, "that what you two and Gretchin have been saying is morally based. That's what you meant when you said *needed to be destroyed* or *rescued*. And Mary too, and Gretchin agreed with you."

"Correct," replied Coldgrave. "But we were responding to your morally charged questions."

"So, you think morally?"

"Yes," she returned, "any time I wish to. Or if you like, the answer is a straight-up yes, but on my terms."

"So, Leonard," he said, leaning back against the cushions, "did you consider any of these things during the execution of the project?"

Packard pulled at his nose. "Hell no, never do. I'm just worried about trapping a misfire in the cylinder. The other half of the time, I'm shooting the bastard for fun or for practice or whatever. Look, I've got a pretty good sense of things, and I'm happy with the system I'm working in, or I wouldn't be working in it. So, yeah, there's my answer, sport, Merry Christmas."

Willard nodded. "How about you, Bradley, we haven't heard from you. Do you agree with what Mary said?"

A sniff. "Right, um, what did she say?"

"Well, she talked about the value difference between the man and the chimps you folks rescued and about how the targets had forfeited their societal value. Do you agree with that?"

"Sure, that sounds good. What's the problem anyway? That's what we're doing here, right, saving the country?"

Bobbie Lee tipped her bottle toward Bradley. "I'd like to know what the problem is mysilf, Brad boy." Then she said to Willard, "I mean, three bodies, three bags, and a jug of bleach to clean it all up, what's to discuss? Tellya what I'm gonna have a problim with, Bob, if you people ain't payin' me regular. You know, I do this shit for money and for fun. The fun's my responsibility, but the money's yours. I'm gonna be checkin' my account, bub, so don't be late."

He looked at her, then at Sandy, who had laid her hand on his arm again.

CHAPTER 22

As her door was opened Connors rolled away, grabbed her clock, then muttered sleepily, "Hey."

Bobbie Lee, on crutches, leaned against the doorframe. Her eyes moved over the pearl skin and up to the mussed hair. "How'd you know it was me?"

Rolling back, "Nobody opens me dar wethout knockin', 'cept you."

"Well, you can't blame 'em, ever'body knows you're a crazy, trigger-happy bloodletter. Come on, git up, girl, it's Chris'mas."

Blinking, then returning the clock to the nightstand, "Go fuck yoursalf, loike, et's only noine, whech is an ungodly hour ef there ever was one."

Putting her weight on the crutches again, "Don't be so profane. Jist for that, I'm leavin' your door wide open, the whole world's gonna see your tits." And hobbling away, she called back, "Git yoursilf up, or I'm gonna drink your coffee."

Connors reached under her pillow for the .38, then got up and pushed the door closed. For a moment she did not move, but stood naked, her bare feet drawing up cold from the planks. She liked having a cold floor there instead of a rug, for it reminded her of Ireland and the coarse years of her childhood.

At the bottom of the stairs, Bobbie Lee set the crutches aside, dropped into the wheelchair, then wheeled herself toward the dining room and the smells of Maggie's breakfast. Gretchin and Bradley squabbled as she rolled up to the table, and Packard muttered to himself over a newspaper article. Maggie, coming from the kitchen, set a platter of hot cinnamon buns on a mat at the center of the table.

"Hey," said Bobbie Lee, "this reminds me of growin' up in Tinnessee, this is beautiful. Mirry Chris'mas, ever'body, pass the beer. Jist kiddin', Maggie, I'll have coffee. Bradley, hand me that pot, wouldya?"

"That's quite all right," returned Maggie sweetly. "It's Christmas, so you can even have beer, if that's what you want." She had liked this Tennessee girl from the beginning when she presented herself to the team during the Florida project. She didn't really mind her overt pragmatism or crude speech. In fact, she admired her candor as well as her rocky muscles. With a smile, she queried, "Is Kelly coming down soon?"

"Yep. I woke miss Sinn Fein up and left her there stark naked with an open door. She'll be here any minute, is my guess."

Bradley and Packard looked up at the mention of Connors being naked. Gretchin watched for a response in Bradley's eyes, but Maggie merely frowned, as if to say a more tasteful remark would have been welcome.

Smacking her lips at the coffee, Bobbie Lee said, "Now, Len, I shouldn't be wishin' you Mirry Chris'mas, you do that Hanukkah thing, don't you, with all them candlesticks and stuff, or whatever they do?"

"Not me," he returned, "I'm fine with every holiday there is, as long as there's whiskey and pie."

She gave the table a little slap. "Too bad Mary had to go off to New York. She's a great girl, and I'm gonna miss her for the party."

Packard grunted, "She won't be missing our party, I think. That money-crowd family of hers does parties to beat the band."

"Beat the band, beat the band—now, what does that mean? Old people say that, don't they?"

He chuckled at this, for he too was fond of this Southern girl.

Throwing a glance toward the doorway as Connors came in, Bobbie Lee said, "Here she is, the irreligious truant."

The other, running a hand through her hair and pulling a chair out, merely sat, then reached for her cup.

"I hate blond hair," said Bobbie Lee, giving her nose a quick swipe with the back of her hand.

"What's wrong with me hair?"

With a roll of her eyes, "Well, it's awful pritty, and if it's pritty, you ought to run a brush through it now and then."

Ignoring this, Connors reached for the cozied pot, filled the cup, then gave it a little slurp. "Mother of God, t'at's joost what I needed."

"See there," said Gretchin to Bobbie Lee, "Kelly's not irreligious."

"T'at's roight," chimed Connors, "and I'm not truant neither, I had to take a pess."

January 2017

Coldgrave shut the Bentley's engine down and sat for a moment as Sibelius' fifth drew to a close. The gloom of the Estate's old stable seemed fitting for the finale of the symphony. She closed her eyes for joy as the music finished. Then she opened them, as if to reality. It was funny, she mused, drawing a deep breath, how life could play with you, within moments ushering you from joy to misery.

Methodically she removed a glove, touched the screen, drew the glove on again, then grabbed her bag and got out. Wrinkling her nose at the unpleasant contrast between the Bentley's soft white and the brash yellow of Bradley's Corvette, she left the garage and walked toward the Big House.

"I haven't been away that long," she protested as Maggie hugged her, then took her coat.

"No, but we missed you anyway."

"Two weeks, that's all, or has it been a month? And I missed everyone. It's so good to be home."

Maggie smiled. "A week and a half, actually."

Coldgrave plucked a dog hair from the sleeve of her sweater. "Well, one loses track of time. And how was everyone's holiday?"

"Christmas was very nice."

"Oh yes, it was Christmas, wasn't it?"

Closing the closet door. "I refreshed your stock, added the Scotch you requested, and got you a new ice bucket. The Nolet's was almost gone, so I finished it and put up a new bottle."

"Yes, of course, thanks, Maggie." And turning back on the stairs, "Dinner at fivish?"

"I should let everyone know," said Coldgrave, after dessert had been served, "Bob is coming on Saturday to lay out a new project. He said he hoped it wasn't too soon to give us more work."

Apart from a groan from Gretchin, there was no response to this announcement. Then Connors broke the silence.

"He won't be gattin' no boike on t'is one."

Bobbie Lee took her finger from her nose, then said, "Don't be sure he won't ask. I wouldn't put it past him to suggist it, since it's only the dead of winter. I still got my right lig to crank it, but you'd have to help me hold it up at the lights."

Coldgrave reached for her glass, then gave it a shake. "Anything from the doctors?"

"Yeah, I gave 'em a call. You'd think they'd call me, but no way. Wraps come off in a couple weeks. After that, I'll jist need a little good whiskey and some exercise."

Wiping his mouth, Packard cast an eye toward her. "How's the 19 doin'?"

"Not bad, Lin," she replied, "thanks for cleanin' it. I ain't an invalid, you know, but thanks."

"Invalid?" said Connors with rare levity. "No, she can stell drenk."

"Anyway," said Coldgrave, "he didn't give me any details."

"I jist hope," said Bobbie Lee, "he doesn't keep tryin' to git us to love the people we kill for him. How stupid can you git. One of these days that man's gonna offend me, and I'm gonna kill mysilf another Yankee."

"Don't do et," said Connors, "or you'll fuck up your pansion, and the man's not worth et."

"I wouldn't let ole Bob get to you," said Packard, "the world needs people like that. I don't, but the world does."

CHAPTER 23

On Saturday afternoon Willard and a sidekick the team had met previously strode into the living room and without formality plopped themselves onto the couch. With amiable expressions they looked expectantly toward Maggie.

"Look at tham," Connors whispered, nudging Bobbie Lee with an elbow, "waitin' to be stoofed weth cookies, loike a couple of pegs."

When Maggie began pouring everyone tea, Coldgrave cleared her throat gently, then said, "All right, so, Bob, would you like to tell us about the new project?"

"Certainly, thank you, Mary," he returned. Somehow the absence of her usual welcome and more formal introduction made him clack his cup and saucer. Momentarily he said, "Well, I hope everyone had a good Christmas."

Gretchin gave her nose a scratch. "No gifts from the Agency though, right?"

"Uh, no, Gretchin," he replied, his tone as personable as he could make it. "To my knowledge, they've never given gifts to employees. They just don't do that kind of thing."

"We know."

He looked at her. He had intended not to let things start this way. "Well," he replied meekly, "there you have it, then. Anyway—"

He was cut short, his mouth partly open, when Packard abruptly reached into his sport jacket, pulled one of the Smiths from its holster, and then casually swung its cylinder out. Although everyone else, who had witnessed the ritual countless times, simply took it in stride, Willard watched silently attentive as the cylinder, after being given a couple of friendly spins, was closed and the piece was leisurely returned to the jackass rig. As the irascible gunman, his eyes upon no one, then merely smacked his lips with satisfaction and folded his arms, Willard swallowed, regained his composure and continued.

"I, uh, I do have a new project to present to the team," he said, reaching for his tea. "That is, if everyone isn't too tired from all the recent work."

"Tired?" returned Gretchin, cocking her head. "Just the other day we killed three people for you, and one of us took two rifle bullets through the leg." And emphasizing the sarcasm, "So, yeah, we're not tired, line 'em up, pop."

If he could wish for anything, it would be power to deal with this woman. Clearing his throat, he said, "I know Ms. Henry needs time to convalesce, I'm aware of that, Gretchin. Don't sell me short, I'm not so insensitive. I'm not asking Ms. Henry to participate. The rest of you—everyone except Bobbie Lee—will have only two targets on this one. The project should be fairly simple to execute, but it could be dangerous too."

Coldgrave, noticing that Packard had begun to doze, lowered her glass. "Any specifics, Bob, as to their weapons?"

Packard blinked at this and looked up. He could sleep through virtually any social situation, especially if it involved discussion. Discussion *per se*, as he often put it, simply bored him. Any mention of weapons, however, would immediately bring his snooze to a close. From his youth he had loved weaponry, especially small arms, and more especially handguns. For him, a handgun, whether revolver or semiautomatic, was more a work of art than a tool, something to be appreciated for its own character. In fact, he considered a handgun's nature to be somewhat organic.

"Well, yes," Willard replied, as if grateful for any friendly query. "Intel says you could encounter quite a number of handguns, as well as expertise in their use. A local gun range has reported that they practice regularly with a whole caseful of semi-autos and that they're good with them, extremely fast and accurate. That's why I said dangerous. But the range only allows lane shooting, so the practice has been limited to that. Your targets will be a man and a woman, both in their forties. They're living in a rented house in Philadelphia."

"That's good to hear," put in Gretchin, "that way, the Agency won't have to put us up in another dumpy motel, which could be expensive, especially if we had to stay more than one night."

Bradley shifted on his chair and brought his foot to his knee. "Come on, Gretch, leave him alone, just let the man talk, okay?"

Willard then sat forward and brought his hands together. "So, the particulars are in the report I'll leave with Mary. Intel is quite detailed. Surveillance has provided a number of photos, even a few eight-by-ten color prints. The window for completing the project is one week, basically five days from tomorrow."

Bradley, who had been playing with his shoestring, put his chin up. "What'd they do?"

"Uh, that I can't tell you." And with a sympathetic shrug, "I simply don't know."

With a grin, albeit an unhappy one, "They don't want us to moralize, huh?"

Another shrug. "I have no idea, Bradley."

Still grinning, then taking to his shoestring again, "Whatever. I guess I'd be the only one to do that, anyway, right?"

He took a sip of his tea. "I think you're on it there, Bradley, right on the money."

Maggie, looking askance at Willard, said sweetly, "You have somewhat of a problem with us, don't you, Bob? I mean, as to our views, our values, or however you might wish to put it."

The candor caught him, and for a moment he merely met her piercing eyes. But their cat-like green soon forced him to look away. "I suppose I do."

"How so?"

"I don't know, I guess I wouldn't quite know how to put it."

And now, not so sweetly, "Try, would you?"

He could not help licking his lips, for all eyes were upon him. "I don't know," he replied meekly. "I'm part of the system, you guys don't seem to be. You work for the system professionally, and in that way you're in it, I admit. But you don't seem to value the system, not the way I do, anyway, you don't seem to appreciate the Agency or your relationship with it, if I'm putting it the right way. . . . Frankly, it's your independence that I find objectionable sometimes."

"Hey," piped Bradley, complaint in his voice. "You can't say that about me, *I'm* playing ball."

"I'm sure," said Willard cautiously, "that you all have sound, uh, values, as you say. It's just that each of you seems to be making them up for himself, if I can put it that way."

Maggie smiled, cocking her head a bit. "You would consider Bradley, of course, to be someone more like you and part of your system."

"That's fair to say, I think. You okay with that, Bradley?"

As Bradley nodded his assent Maggie continued, "So, the rest of us, you would see as somewhat antinomian, then?"

He nodded, staring at her, as if to suppress a chuckle at a gross understatement. "Of course," he replied.

"And existentialist?"

"Yes, of course. . . . I haven't offended anyone, I hope." Then he looked at Coldgrave. "Mary?"

Lowering her glass. "No, not at all. In what way should I be offended, Bob?"

"Well, by having me place you in that category."

She looked at him. "And have you done that, Bob, have you placed me there? Should I feel that I have been moved and put someplace?"

"I don't understand."

"It doesn't matter. . . . If you need to categorize me, Bob, feel free to do so, I won't be offended."

"Well," put in Gretchin impatiently, "you don't need to ask if you've offended me, Bob, I can't remember a thing you've ever said or done that hasn't offended me. If you want to stick a label on me, go ahead. I've got labels I stick on you every time I see you."

To quell the impulse to tell her to drop dead, really dead, he drew a breath, counted to five, then let it out. It was a new technique he had for dealing with stress and anger—not just counting to five, but holding his breath at the same time. So far, it was helping. He smiled at her, then turned to Packard and queried, "Len?"

With a croaking sound, Packard cleared his throat. "Philosophy's pretty much useless to me, pal. I carry mine in my holster, anyway."

Willard nodded. "I understand, right. . . . And you, Bobbie Lee, how about you?"

"I agree with Lin here," she replied, running a finger along the side of her nose. "And I don't have a problem with terms or labels or categories or whatever the hell else people wanna use to say what they think about me. I've got my Confederate flag nailed to my wall, jist like you've got your Union flag nailed to yours. So, call me whatever you want, I'm good with it."

His gaze went to Connors. Swallowing, he said, "Kelly?"

After a moment, "I don't give a fuck what you call me, unlass et bothers me. I joost do what I want."

He let his eyes go closed briefly. Then, as if to complete the circle, he looked to Maggie. Her eyes seemed to be kind, her smile sweet, her whole demeanor gentle. Somehow he felt good, satisfied that he had put some of his anxiety into words.

But as he looked at her she dropped the smile and asked, "And what term should we use for you, Bob?" As this seemed to catch him off guard, she added, "Philosophically, that is."

Again he brought his hands together. "I'm not sure. I suppose I look at life pretty much the same way as Bradley does. I see things as either right or wrong, and I'm a patriot."

She did not query further, but touched her cheek lightly with a finger, then offered him a little smile, as if to say she considered the conversation finished.

Accepting this, he sat back and let his gaze rest briefly upon them one by one. What a pathetic, macabre menagerie! If he had indeed gone into the ministry, would his congregation have been anything like this? Maggie, clearly the more acceptable of the lot, with her cookies and tea, polite to the point of being pathologically civil. Packard, the old wolf, with his silly sport coat bulging from his magnums. Bradley, with his goofy shoestring fixation or whatever it was, but at heart so much like himself. Then Gretchin, with her slanderous talk and incessant display of disrespect. What a wretched, pain of a human being—nice to look at, but terrible to encounter.

The Henry woman, with her rocky muscles, her Confederate-flag mentality. Connors, with her ghostlike eyes, her awful penchant for killing. And Mary, with her guru expertise in weaponry and ballistics, and nothing but alcohol in her veins. He let the gaze linger upon her. To think that he had been attracted to her, actually romantically attracted. Certainly she possessed a beauty most women would die for. But what had he seen in her beyond that, ever to be drawn to her?

CHAPTER 24

Bobbie Lee arched her back, then adjusted the pillows behind her. "Actually," she said, reaching to the nightstand for her glass of Jack on ice, "what I'm missin' lately is the weight liftin'. The prissure'd be too great, the doc said. Gotta give it a couple weeks more. But then," here she tipped the glass at Connors, "it's rock and roll."

"Batter watch your stap, you could lemp loike a shot dog for the rast of your loife."

"My drink's low, pass the bottle."

Bobbie Lee watched as Connors first added another half inch to her own glass, then handed over the bottle. There was a candid pragmatism about this Irish woman that she could not resist. Often she found herself recalling how they had first met on the Jacksonville project. How the door had been opened and the colorless eyes had seemed so eerie as to glow. How later the beauty of the skin and body had been so off-putting as to reach into her mind and capture her. How the ability to kill had been so keen as to be mesmerizing.

"Hey, tell me somethin'," she said, her eyes moving over the blond hair, the fair skin, "you ever think about philosophy and stuff, like what Willard said?"

Connors shook her head. "Not much. What's the good of et?"

With a shrug, "Maybe it leads somewhere."

"Et goes en circles, loike relegion."

Swirling her whiskey over the ice, "Well, you don't seem to have much use for either, girl, that's for sure. . . . So, are you ready for this project?"

Connors reached for the bottle. "What's to be ready for? Et's joost kellin'."

"Now, there you go philosophizin'. Maybe I was wrong. I guess now you're gonna pull out a rosary—but then, you'd rather count bullets than beads, right?"

Connors drained her glass, then looked at her. "You're talkin' nonsanse."

"Guess I am. I think I jist need to keep you here. You looked like you were gittin' the itch to leave. I need somebody to talk to. This tore-up lig feels like a goddamn whale."

With a grin, "Hurts?"

"Yes, it does. Hand me them meds on the drisser top."

"Water?"

"Naw, this is good enough."

"Suit yoursalf, but I don't need a Tannessee carpse on me hands."

Bobbie Lee held the glass up and looked through the amber liquid. After washing the pain killers down she said, "And jist what would you do if I did die?"

"I don't know, gat Mary to call Wellard, I guess, to steck you en a body bag."

Taking a seat, she pushed back to balance on the chair's rear legs. She didn't mind staying, even though it was late. She didn't mind talking either. She liked this Tennessee woman, if *like* was the word. Seldom in her life had she been able to say she loved someone. She looked at the pretty but not glamorous face, the yellow, wolf-like eyes, the long, straight, chestnut hair. Often she found herself recalling how they had first met on the Jacksonville project. How in security mode she had opened the front door only to be disarmed by the yellow eyes, the chestnut hair. Sometimes she dreamed of how, on the Texas project, they had ridden the motorcycle to rescue the boy. How Bobbie Lee had cranked the Triumph, then told her to get up behind. How Packard had handed her the magnum just before they launched, saying that she needed a real gun and reminding her she had not six but seven shots. How at high speed they had molded themselves to the bike to go faster. How they had caught the car, and Bobbie Lee, with incredible skill, had run them up beside the window for the best shot. How she herself had leveled the magnum and blown the man to fucking hell. And how, after pulling the boy from the wrecked car, they had put him between them on the bike and taken him back safe to his mother.

Bobbie Lee rubbed her leg. "That sounds to me like you've got a cold heart, girl. Jist lit them zip me up and cart me off, huh?"

"T'at's roight." And bringing the front legs of the chair down, "So, ef you catch a .223 en the head instead of the lag, what should I do weth you?"

Shifting her leg and wincing, "I don't know, cremate me, I guess—jist douse me with whiskey and light me up. And you'd be cold enough to do it, wouldn't you? I know you're cold, girl, I've seen how you kill people, like a red-hot dragon with a cold, cold heart."

"I don't feel cold, and I love me ma."

"Well, hallelujah, you've got somethin' inside, then. Is she the only one you love?"

Connors looked at her, then answered, "No."

"Goddammit, this lig hurts! I hate gittin' shot. Come on, talk to me here, the meds ain't kickin' in. And pour me some more Jack, would you?"

After pouring more whiskey for them, Connors said, "You're gonna have more scars than me."

"Nobody's got more scars than you. You are one scarred up lady, I could be a witness to that. And you watch yoursilf on this here projict, I don't want one of them targits hittin' the jackpot."

Connors stuck a forefinger into her drink, gave the whiskey and ice a swirl, then put the dripping finger into her mouth to suck off the liquid. "Don't worry, loike," she replied, "I'll be careful."

"Bet you're glad not to have to ride on the Harley."

"Aye, et's too fuckin' cold."

"I should be outta these here bandages and ready to roll, come spring."

"I loikes the camper."

The yellow eyes glistened, then met the color-less eyes. "The Acadia trip was real nice, wasn't it? Think I'll spend my time here convalescin' pickin' us out a new place to go to. We gotta see the rist of the country, girl."

Bradley depressed the power button, then set the remote on the nightstand. "Know what I like about John Wayne?"

"I can't imagine."

"Ah, come on, guess. And don't pick on me, just guess."

"Let's see, his swagger?"

"Nope, not even close."

"I don't want to guess anymore, Bradley, just tell me. And turn that light out."

"I like it that he never shot anybody in the back. And that's a fact, too. He refused to make movies where he had to shoot somebody in the back. How about that?"

"And that's a good thing?"

Switching off the lamp, "Of course."

"Sure, sure, I can work through that, just let me think about it."

"Come on, you're being sarcastic. It is a good thing, it's honorable. You want me to be honorable as a husband, don't you? ... Gretchin, are you asleep?"

"No."

"Well?"

She pulled the blanket up to her ear. "To a degree, I suppose. But you could overdo it."

"Well, I don't think John Wayne overdid it."

"My guess is," she replied yawning, "if John Wayne refused to do a movie where he had to shoot somebody in the back, it wasn't so much because of his honor as his ego—you know, big, blabbering, swaggering ego."

"How can you say that?"

"Ego is always idealistic or romantic, never realistic."

He moved next to her and slipped his arm over her, gently grasped her breast, then kissed her neck through her hair. "You want me to be romantic, don't you?"

"To a degree, I suppose," she murmured. "But you could overdo it."

Maggie took a seat beside her husband, then leaned against him. "What channel is that?"

"I don't know," he grunted, "some house sales thing."

"Oh, I love those," she returned, reaching for a chip. "And we should watch it. We'll need to retire for real sometime."

He looked at her. "Feeling your age?"

"Feeling it and thinking about it."

"Sure you want to do that?"

"Seventy-two years old," she returned, "and I'm not supposed to think about my age? God, Lenny, please."

"Hell, I'm sixty-eight, that's not too far behind you. You don't catch me screwin' my mind up about it."

She took another chip, then pointed it at the screen. "Isn't that beautiful? That would be perfect for us."

"We don't have that kind of money. I did in my youth, but I spent it all on women, beer, and ammunition."

"Oh-h," she groaned, "you old bastard. But what do you think, shouldn't we start looking for a place where we can spend our last years together?"

He downed the rest of his Scotch, then chewed a piece of the ice. "Sure, what the hell, go ahead and look for something if you want."

"It doesn't seem to be urgent for you."

A sigh. "I always figured I'd never reach retirement age."

"Yeah, yeah, but now that you've survived this long, well, how about it? A little place in Florida maybe? And why are you drinking that stuff?"

He peered into the glass. "I'm not anymore, it's empty."

She gave his knee a gentle slap. "I saved a bottle, you old drunk, hold on. And give me that glass." A minute later she returned with a fresh drink. "Here you go, on Mary's party ice, crystal clear. Now, tell me I don't love you."

"You're a trooper, woman, what can I say?"

"How about something romantic?"

He pulled her close and gave her a squeeze. "I love the hell out of you, you know that?"

"I do," she replied softly. "And likewise."

Coldgrave closed the book and set it aside, wondering why she had wanted to read it in the first place. Aimlessly she reached for the remote, depressed the power button, then leaned back against the pile of pillows on her bed. Did drinking to pictures take her further away than drinking to words? Hitting the mute button, she watched as the images moved in their charade. Closing her eyes, she held down the channel selector, then released it and opened her eyes to see what luck had given her. With a sigh of disappointment, she depressed the power button again, then closed her eyes. Perhaps it was just better to drink and think.

Getting up to refresh her drink, she wondered why memories seemed important, since they made such an inaccurate bridge to reality. Memories were always available, but they were never accurate.

Not bothering to discard the empty bottle of Bombay Sapphire, she looked over the array of gins, scotches, bourbons, vodkas, brandies, absinthes, cognacs, rums, tequilas, liqueurs, the amarettos, vermouths, cointreaus, the bitters, the drambuies. Taking up a fresh glass, she added ice from the bucket, then reached for the Nolet's.

In the mirror behind the bottles she looked at her image and into the past. The memories are inaccurate, she mused, but so is the image that elicits them. It was the self, not the image, that had initially made the events that would become the memories. Her right eye took in the hair in the image, then the nose, the lips, the neck, the breasts. She had been told many times that she was beautiful. But had any such comment ever been important to her? If not, why now was she looking to her image to elicit the memories? Turning from the image, but not from herself, she returned to the bed and took up the book again.

CHAPTER 25

Philadelphia, January

"Now, whose idea was this?" queried Bobbie Lee with a snicker. Giving the SUV more power to pass a slow-moving truck, she said, "I think it was my idea, wasn't it?"

Behind her, Packard replied, "Bradley sure didn't argue with you. I think he was thinking of it himself."

"Yeah, he loves drivin' that Corvette around, like he's a famous playboy or somethin'"

"Oh, I'd say just a football player, that'll do."

"Well, he'd tellya at least the quarterback."

Connors, also in the back seat, queried, "How's the lag?"

Tightening her grip on the wheel, "Doin' fine, don't worry."

"But I am worryin', loike."

"Well, don't be. If I need meds, I'll take 'em tonight. Right now I'm good."

Coldgrave pulled her mirror down, touched the corner of her mouth with a gloved finger, then carefully applied more lipstick. "Just be ready to take over at the wheel, Len," she said. Experience had taught her what serious pain could do to anyone's resolve.

"Don't worry, Mary," said Bobbie Lee, "I'll be stayin' right here."

Coldgrave looked at the highway before them. "Kelly, ask them where they are."

Moments later, Connors replied, "She says they're en an argumant."

Not bothering to hide her annoyance, "Is that really what she said?"

"Aye."

"Please tell her I said not to answer that way."

Connors obeyed. "She says we should see tham behoind us soon."

With a sigh, "Thank you, Kelly."

Checking her mirror, Bobbie Lee said, "I see 'em. Sure can't miss that gaudy color. That car's like a whore on four wheels."

"I like Philadelphia," said Bradley as he accelerated to keep close to the SUV.

After a moment, "Okay, I'll play, why do you like Philadelphia?"

"Because it's got a major team in all the sports."

"I thought you were going to say it's where you proposed to me."

"Sure, that too, absolutely. All of which means that we *both* should like this city. Agreed?"

"No, Bradley. No, I don't agree."

He tapped the wheel. "Come on, loosen up. I'm just making small talk, to get you off the argument."

She looked at him. "Me? To get *me* off the argument?"

"Well, you started it, you have to admit."

"I didn't start anything."

"Okay, okay, I'll let you have this one—you did not start the argument. It wasn't your fault that we've been arguing the whole time we've been in the car, how's that? Satisfied? I'm the bad guy."

"No, you're not the bad guy, you're the stupid guy. Or—or—you're just the guy, since the adjective *stupid* is redundant there, isn't it? You're the guy, that's all, the guy. And you're not stupid, Bradley, or insensitive, you're just a *guy*, a goddamn guy."

"You don't have to be profane, Gretchin."

"Just fucking shut up, please. And turn the goddamn heat down, I'm very hot now."

He did not respond further, but simply reached to adjust the temperature control. What had he said, what had he done? The whole trip—misery. It was always the same, they couldn't drive five miles without fighting. Now, if he didn't hear her voice for the rest of the day, he would be happy. Then he heard her voice.

"Okay," she said, "Red Lion Road's next, I'm texting them. Get in the exit lane, don't miss it." And as he obeyed she texted, *Breaking off. See you there.*

Making the turn, he said, "I can't believe all these people are out."

"They're shopping, moron, don't worry about it. There aren't that many anyway. Besides, it'll be another ten minutes or so."

"I always worry about it. Mary isn't going to, that's for sure. And Kelly, Bobbie Lee, even Len, they don't care. They'd all just pull out their guns and blast away, no matter how many people were watching."

"Here, look at this, it's getting more residential."

"But it's broad daylight."

"It's January, Bradley, it's winter, for God's sake. Most people are inside. Stop being paranoid."

Minutes later Bobbie Lee brought the SUV to the curb and left the engine running.

"That's the house," said Coldgrave. "That's the car in the report."

Bobbie Lee, her eyes on the street, gave her leg a quick rub. "Bradley jist turned onto the street, about two blocks away."

Coldgrave watched as the Corvette came toward them from the opposite direction, then drew up at the curb across the street.

"Don'tcha love the suburbs?" said Bobbie Lee. "You can jist park anywhere."

Coldgrave gave an aristocratic sniff. "Quaint, the suburbs are quaint."

"Jesus! I'd hate to hear what you'd say about Tinnessee. The whole world can't be jist mansions and fancy parties, you know."

"Certainly. I did not mean to imply that it should."

Then Connors said, "Gratchin joost taxted they're ready."

Coldgrave flipped her mirror down, took a look at her lipstick, then flipped it back up. "So are we," she replied. And drawing the .38 from her purse, she put it into her coat pocket, then said, "Pass me the pump, please." Then taking the shotgun and propping it against the dash, "All right, Kelly, text them we're set."

Moments later Connors said, "Confairmed, they're sat."

Pulling the .38 from her pocket, Coldgrave said, "Whatever these people did, it warranted extensive surveillance, we've never had such detailed intel. I only hope it proves helpful, I'd hate to have to storm that house."

"It's four-thirty," said Bobbie Lee, looking at the dash clock. "If the intel's right, they should be comin' out right about now. I hope Gritchin's watchin' from her angle, instead of jist fightin' with Bradley." A moment later, her eyes fixed on the side door of the house, she said, "Here we go, look at this, right on time. Imagine goin' out to a restaurant every single day, and at the same time, and bein' so regular about it that you're jist tellin' the whole world to track your ass."

As the woman walked around to the passenger's side of the car the man closed the inner door to the house, checked it multiple times, and closed the storm door. Then he got in beside her and started the engine. For a few second they sat, apparently waiting for the engine to warm up.

When the car backed down the driveway and into the street, then headed toward the SUV,

Coldgrave said, "Down." After the car had passed and they had sat up again, the Corvette was just passing Bobbie Lee's window in pursuit. Coldgrave gave the command to go, and Bobbie Lee dropped the shift, accelerated, and drove to the end of the block. There she made a right, circled the block and soon brought them up behind the Corvette.

"Stick to plan," said Coldgrave, her gloved hand gripping the .38, "they block the car, wait for them, stay close."

Bobbie Lee replied, "Wouldn't do nothin' else, lady."

"This area's perfect," uttered Coldgrave. "Kelly, get her on the phone."

Half a block later, Connors said, "Gratchin, stay on the phone. Mary's gonna call et."

One by one, the three cars stopped at the corner, then accelerated into the next block. In the SUV all seatbelts except Bobbie Lee's were off and all weapons were out. Coldgrave, moving closer to the windshield for the best view, said suddenly, "Next corner, this is it. Tell her."

Connors gave the command into the phone, then dropped it onto the seat beside her. As the three cars neared the corner the Corvette moved to pass the targets' car and the SUV accelerated to close the gap.

"Go now!" commanded Gretchin inside the Corvette.

Bradley put his foot down and shot them past the targets' car, then jerked the wheel right and slammed on the brakes to make the block. The man in the car, apparently surprised, simply stopped in front of Gretchin's door, unaware the SUV had blocked him from behind. He cracked his door to get out.

But Gretchin did not wait for him and was out and now walking toward him. As he pushed the door open and got out she pulled the 9mm from her coat pocket, with Connors and Packard advancing from the SUV. And when seeing the gun he instantly whirled to get back into the car. Gretchin halted, brought the gun to level, and fired, shooting him in the side. Packard fired, also, from the opposite direction, knocking him against the inside of the door and dropping him to his knees. As the heavy shots from the magnum continued to slam into him the woman, bawling out horrific screams, pushed opened her door and put a leg out. But Connors was there and shot her in the face twice, so that she fell out of the car and down upon the asphalt. Then Connors fired twice again, into the back of the woman's head. At the other door Packard stood over the crumpled, still man, reholstered the empty Smith, then drew the second and fired into the man's head, blowing part of the skull away. At nearly the same time, Connors fired her fifth shot, into the woman's head.

Slowly Coldgrave got out, casually walked up to Connors, and looked down at the woman's mangled head. Without a word, she moved around to the driver's side and looked down at the riddled man. When Gretchin, looking over the window frame at the mess, queried if it was done Coldgrave merely gave a nod. And when Packard asked if she wanted him to switch their engine off she answered with a single shake of her head.

A man, standing at the railing of his porch, who had witnessed the entire incident, pulled his front door open and went inside. On the other side of the street, two women, who had been strolling along the sidewalk and had gone down upon the grass to huddle together when the shooting started, sat crying and hugging each other. A boy and girl, both in their early teens, who had turned the corner near the Corvette just as Gretchin fired, now stood watching as the team returned to the cars.

When all were inside, Bobbie Lee, moved the shift down but waited until the Corvette had made a right at the corner. Then she drove around the car, with its open doors and oozing corpses, and at the corner prepared to make a left. "Look at that girl," she chuckled, glancing at the teenagers, "hand on her mouth like she's never seen anyone shot b'fore. Now, that's an example, I'm jist sayin', of a sheltered kid." Then she made the turn and drove away.

"How's the lag?" queried Connors.

"Could be worse," Bobbie Lee answered. "Beer would make it better, that's for sure." As the SUV left the neighborhood, she said to Coldgrave, "That was entertaining, but it wasn't much of a shootout. I expicted these people to throw some lead at us."

But Coldgrave, who had opened her phone, did not reply. "Hello, Bob, everything's done. We're heading out now. . . . No one hurt, no. . . . Surely, just a moment. . . ."

They listened as she gave him the intersection streets for the cleanup crew, as she said goodbye, and as she sighed just before slipping the phone back into the purse. They followed her movements as she performed the ritual of pulling the visor down and checking the lipstick.

"We certainly haven't had much of a winter," she said.

Bobbie Lee snickered. "It's all that global warmin'. They say the polar bears are starvin'."

"I'm not complaining," put in Packard. "I hate movin' snow, even with a snowblower. I'm getting too old for it." And when Coldgrave had passed him the shotgun and he had put it behind his seat, he added, "I think I'll retire, this time for real, I'm getting too old for this shit."

Bobbie Lee drew a hand across her nose. "For movin' snow?"

"No," he answered, "for draining people."

"I don't know, think of all the fun you'll miss. You got to empty a gun into a man today, how're you gonna live without that?"

"Are you kidding?" he returned, stretching out his arm. "Do you know how many jackets, and shirts too, I've ruined getting blood on me? No, I'm gonna love retirement. Just look at Kelly here. Powder blue coat, very nice, probably cost a lot— look at all that blood and shit—totally ruined."

"Et dedn't cost mooch," said Connors, "t'at's why I wore et. Ef et doesn't come out en the wash, I'll joost toss et."

Then everyone was silent, and Coldgrave looked out her window with a sigh.

"You're quiet today, Mary," said Bobbie Lee, "you seem a little melancholy."

"Oh," replied Coldgrave with another sigh, "not at all. . . . But perhaps I am feeling a little parched. What does everyone think—perhaps a stop?"

CHAPTER 26

The Estate

"What's the use of that kind of thinking?" asked Willard as he sat alone on the couch a week later. "You killed them brutally, with no apparent point to the brutality. That's not professional. You carried it out in a residential area, on a public street and near an intersection, all as if you didn't care that innocent people might see it or even be physically hurt. Bullets do stray, you know. And in fact a number of people did see it. For instance, a teenage boy and girl actually stood and watched the whole thing. The girl was only thirteen, the boy fourteen. Neither will ever be the same, I'm sure." And placing both hands on his head, he looked down at the floor.

"Actually," said Gretchin, "nobody will ever be the same."

His brow furrowing, "What?"

"Just what I said, nobody will ever be the same. Think about it."

He swallowed, as if to quell his anger. "How is that helpful?"

"It isn't," she returned, "it wasn't meant to be. You just want things to be done in an orthodox way."

"What's wrong with that?"

"Orthodoxy just gives the illusion that things don't change. You're pushing orthodoxy, you want us to be orthodox. Every time you use the word *professional* that's what you mean."

Pressing his back against the cushions, he stretched his legs out and crossed them. "Who are you saying wants this, Gretchin?"

"You do, the Agency does, the whole goddamn world does. That's how society promotes itself, produces tax payers and soldiers. I wasn't born two years before yesterday, asshole."

Rolling his eyes, "Oh, come on, Gretchin, don't throw that stuff at me, I know the game you're playing. You didn't like the philosophy discussion at the last meeting, so now you're throwing philosophy back at me. That's not helpful, Gretchin, that's spiteful. *And*, you're no philosopher, trust me."

Her eyes narrowed, which made him catch his breath. "Trust you?" she said. "You should be flushed down the tubes, not trusted."

With another roll of his eyes, "Thank you, Gretchin. Thank you for that exquisite imagery. That too is not helpful. The point is, if I can get back to what I was saying—"

"What you were saying," she interjected, "is that you don't like us. Oh, you claim that you don't like our methods, which is pure bullshit. *We* are what you don't like, Bob, we know that. You don't like it that we live outside your definitions. And what especially irks you is that the Agency lets us do it, even pays us to do it."

He closed his eyes. He did not want to look at her. In fact, he wished he could open his eyes and simply not see her—ever again. But when he did open them she was looking right at him, as if prepared to stare him down. Then he said, "I simply wanted to say—that, as a team, you seem to be resisting my efforts to make you more professional, more acceptable. And it's as though you're doing it on purpose. I just don't understand it."

"What I want to know," she said, "is how, after seminary, you escaped the ministry."

He looked at her. "I didn't go to seminary."

"Then you should get the Oscar for best actor. We're not your flock, you know."

He reddened, but then said calmly, "If we could just get back here—please?—please? For instance, could somebody explain to me why you left their car running?"

"Bob," said Maggie, "would you like more tea?"

"What? Uh, no, no, Maggie, thanks. No more right now, thanks."

"Would you care for another cookie, then?"

"No," he nearly stuttered, "I'm fine, Maggie. It was very good, everything was very good, but I'm fine, I don't need any more right now."

Not giving him a chance to continue, she turned to Coldgrave. "Mary, I'm going to the kitchen for a bowl of chips for everyone. How is your drink?"

As if overcome with frustration, he laid the back of his hand on his forehead. "Listen," he said, making no attempt to mask his anxiety, "I would like to finish my thought, if I may. Do we really need chips?"

Her mouth fell open. "Oh, of course we do," she returned indignantly, "and Mary's drink needs refreshing. It'll only take a minute."

With that, she took the glass from Coldgrave and left. He watched her, turned back to the others, then sank deeper into the cushions. He had driven himself, but now wished he had brought someone if only for the empathy. To make things worse, Gretchin had sensed his aloneness.

"What's the matter, Bob," she queried contemptuously, "the Agency too cheap to pay for a driver this trip?"

He wanted to tell her to just shove her snide comments. Instead, he replied, "They're not cheap at all, in my opinion. I wanted to come by myself today, that's all." And defensively he added, "I enjoy driving, I like the time to think. Sometimes I listen to audio books."

"Really? Well, then, you should take along the hard copy sometimes and try reading it as you drive."

Looking away from her, he watched as Maggie returned with the bowl of chips and freshened drink.

"Now," said Coldgrave pleasantly, "Bob, you wanted to finish your thoughts."

But Maggie was holding out the bowl to him. "No," he nearly barked, "no chips, thank you, Maggie, no chips."

"Oh, have one, would you?" she insisted, pushing the bowl closer. "They're tasty."

He took the little plate from her and chose a few chips. Holding the plate with two hands, he looked up at her.

She smiled as she looked down at him, for he seemed so much to resemble a dog in the rain. "And more tea, then?"

His eyes going shut, "Sure, sure, that would be great. It'll keep me awake for the trip home."

"That's the spirit, Bob. We wouldn't want you falling asleep at the wheel, would we?"

Coldgrave, half of the drink now gone, gave the glass a whirl to slosh the gin, and said, "Now, Bob, if you're all set and would like to continue, we're ready to hear what you have to say. As I recall, you were asking about the car."

"Uh, yes, the car. . . . Yes. Actually I wanted to know why it was left running."

"That was my decision," she replied, lowering the glass. "Len had asked if I wanted him to shut the engine off, but I decided to just let it run."

"Why?"

She brought one leg over the other. "There seemed to be too much blood and mess to climb through. I thought he might get it on his coat."

He took a long moment to digest this, his eyes going to Packard's worn and soiled sport coat. "Oh," he returned with a nod. "Well, okay, sure. That's, uh, that's a good explanation. I can see that, I guess."

Gretchin, clearly disappointed that he had been so amenable, thus denying her an opening for an attack, grabbed a handful of her hair and pushed it behind an ear.

Bradley, sensing her aggression, touched her arm. "Just let it go," he said gently, "okay?"

But she turned to him and answered aloud, "No, I won't. He keeps trying to put his goddamn hands on us."

He shrugged. "Please?"

For some reason, she did let it go. Then he took his arm away and smiled at her.

"I did have another thing to add," said Willard. "Actually it's a question concerning safety. It seemed to me after reading Mary's report that the target was between Gretchin and Leonard, that Gretchin fired first, then Leonard, and that you were firing in the direction of each other. Is that correct, did I get that right? Gretchin?"

"Yes."

"Well—what if you had missed or the bullet had gone through him?"

"I'd have probably hit Len, or possibly Mary in the car."

"Why did you shoot, then?"

"That's a stupid question."

He looked at her, then said to Packard, "Why did you fire, Leonard, in the direction of Gretchin, and with Bradley behind her in their car?"

Packard roused himself, for he had been dozing. Straightening up in his chair, he replied, "To kill the man, why the hell else do you think I pull a trigger?"

"No, I mean, why did you do it if it wasn't safe for Gretchin or Bradley?"

"I think, Bob," put in Coldgrave, "that our priority is always killing the targets, not keeping each other safe."

"But safety is very important, it's Agency policy, you all know that. We don't want any of you to be hurt, let alone by each other. I wouldn't want you firing in my direction, Gretchin. And Leonard, that magnum, it gives me chills to think of being anywhere even close to its line of fire."

"I do think," said Coldgrave, "that of all rounds, the .357 is one of the more interesting. Its trajectory is minimal, and it's impact is really amazing. I love the round, myself, although I personally prefer the P+ .38."

Blinking, he returned, "I'm not really talking about the qualities of the round, Mary, but about safety. Let's stick to the point, if we can."

She merely lifted the glass to her lips, then said, "But one wonders what makes someone choose one round over the other, don't you think?"

He blinked again, moving his head from side to side. "Not really, no. My concern, Mary, was about the safety of the team, and also of bystanders. Can we stick to the point please?"

"I thought I was," she returned. "The point was about Leonard's magnum and Gretchin's 9mm, correct?"

"No, it was safety—safety during a very dangerous situation."

"Well, of course, surely, I can see that, fine," she replied pleasantly, holding the glass just before her lips.

His eyelids drooping for a moment, suddenly he became animated and said, "Okay, fine. Now let me ask you this, Mary, since you're considered one of the Agency's gun gurus. Since the target's door was open, as I understand was the case, would either a 9mm or .357 bullet have been dangerous after, say, penetrating the car door?"

"Both hollow-points?" And following a nod from Gretchin and Packard, she said, "I would say as to the 9mm probably yes with the fragments. As to the .357, definitely yes, especially if fragmentation occurred. Hollow-points are meant to expand, you understand. But ballistics is not a science where any prediction is really reliable."

He brightened. "Yes, I know that, but what you're saying is that even bullet fragments would have been dangerous, correct?"

"Oh, certainly. Leonard could easily have been killed by a any shot from Gretchin, either from the bullet or its fragments after, for instance, a ricochet. And the same for Gretchin or Bradley by any shot from Len. Even glass fragments, had the bullets passed through the car's window, would have been dangerous and potentially lethal."

"Well," he said, clapping his hands, "there you have it, the situation was extremely dangerous, which is what I was saying. ... You know," here he shook a forefinger at Gretchin, then at Packard, "I think you two were both a little reckless."

Coldgrave brought the glass to her nose, inhaled the alcohol, then tipped it up and drained it.

"Gretchin," he continued, "don't you think you acted recklessly? I would like a response, if I may have one."

Nonchalantly Gretchin simply raised a hand and gave him the finger.

Undeterred, he addressed Packard. "Leonard?"

Sleepily Packard brought himself to his feet, then simply uttered, "Jesus! I need a cold beer."

They watched as he trundled off to the kitchen. No one spoke until he had returned and taken his seat and was pleasurably chugging the beer.

"I would like to point out," said Willard, his voice softening, "a simple ricochet can kill someone as easily as a straight-on shot."

There was no response from anyone. The only sound in the room seemed to be bubblings and gurglings as Packard drank his beer. Still there was silence when Maggie took up Coldgrave's empty glass and left for the kitchen.

"Ah," said Packard as he finished the bottle, "now I'll sleep like a baby."

Willard looked at them wearily, his gaze resting briefly upon each of them. "Actually," he said, pausing to consider, "I think that's all I wanted to talk to everyone about—I mean, concerning the project. . . . But I do have a piece of good news, so to speak. There's nothing on the slate for this team for at least a month, and the Agency has authorized paid vacation time for everyone." Then, obviously pleased with himself for being the bearer of this news, he cocked his head in expectation of a response.

"So," said Gretchin, "the Agency's paying for our vacations. That's very good news, Bob. And I always thought they were cheap."

Immediately he sat up. "Paid vacation *time,* Gretchin, just the time."

"But we're salaried, vacation time is always paid, so why say it at all?"

His tone icy, "Just to let you know you could go on vacation."

Bradley put his hand on her arm again, then said to Willard, "Thanks, Bob, that's great to know. It'll be good to get away. Guess we'll have to plan something special."

Willard looked at him. Clearly as a good guy he was the most pathetic of the bunch. And *bunch* was the right word, too. What a wretched lot of reptilians, slithering around their stinking lair, their hands practically dripping with fresh blood, joking, laughing, sipping Maggie's pathologically perfect tea, drinking their putrid alcohol! And here was a good guy, a moral man, someone with a genuine soul, a patriot, right in their midst, the example of his sound character apparently having no effect whatever on them. Worse, he had to live with the dragon lady herself and endure the vitriolic heat that incessantly issued from her mouth. Poor stupid man, caught like a beast between his honor and his hormones.

Then, on impulse, he stood. "I should be going," he said, averting his gaze from them. "Enjoy your vacations. I'm sure there will be a new project waiting for you when you're rested up." Here he simply turned from them and walked to the front closet for his coat. Catching up, Maggie pulled the garment from its hanger and helped him on with it, discretely snatching a dog hair from one of its sleeves.

"Now, you take care of yourself, Bob," she said cheerily, "and have a good drive home. Say hi to Sandy for us, she's a sweet thing."

A chill put its hands around his neck as she spoke. He merely replied, "Yes, she is, and I'll tell her you all said hi. Thanks, Maggie."

"Don't forget," called Gretchin from the living room, "if you get sleepy, just keep driving."

CHAPTER 27

"So, what would we do," posed Bradley at dinner that evening, "if we found out in the middle of a project that the people were actually innocent?"

"And how," queried Maggie, setting a fresh pot of tea at the center of the table, "might that knowledge come to us, would you think?"

He shrugged. "I don't know. But what if it did somehow, what should we do?"

Gretchin shook her head. She liked him like this, but she hated him like this, too. Always she had wished that if she were to marry it would be to someone she could be proud of. She had never been proud of this man. He was a genuine man, to be sure, which was something to be proud of, since he had shown his attention to her and eventually asked her to marry him. He was strong, handsome, military. But for as long as she had known him he had possessed the irksome ability to say the most stupid things. "Just eat, Bradley," she said, "please."

"I'm just asking. Can't I ask? It's a good question, think about it. We could find out somehow that a target—a guy, say—was absolutely innocent. . . . Len, how about you, what would you do?"

Clinking her fork, Gretchin put in, "Why are you asking this?"

Another shrug. "I don't know, maybe because it's been bothering me that we weren't told what the last targets had done."

"Oh God, Bradley, really? You've actually been thinking about this?"

He lifted his coffee cup. "I have, I admit. And it bothers me. You were the first one that shot the guy, and you haven't thought about it?"

"Sure I've thought about it," she returned, "but I've thought about it with every project. I think about lots of things, so what? You're killing someone, how could anyone not think about it? But it's part of the work we're in, anybody should be able to see that too."

He looked at Packard. "So, Len, what if you discovered he was innocent, what would you actually do?"

With a grumpy snort that said he had been irritated, Packard looked at him. "I don't know, kill him anyway, I guess. What's the difference? Like she says, it's part of the job."

Bradley gave the knife beside his plate a nudge with his finger. "You wouldn't let him go, that wouldn't be an option?"

"I don't know, I might let him go or I might not, maybe depending on what side of the bed I got out of that day, I'd decide on the spot. What's the difference?"

"I'm sure *he* would think there's a difference."

A grunt. "Life's overrated."

"But not *his* life, not to him anyway."

Coldgrave peered into her glass, then sloshed the liquid over the ice. "I don't know why I wanted whiskey today," she said. "Bradley, don't you think the Agency might have known he was innocent but sent you anyway?"

He hesitated, but then said, "I guess that's possible."

"The men in the minivan weren't guilty of anything, at least according to the Agency. The whole thing was a diplomatic payback."

He looked at her, his eyes earnest. "I know, and that bothered me and still does. I haven't been able to work through it so that I'm okay with it. But that was different, at least from what I'm asking, because *somebody* was guilty, and those men were representatives of their system. Maybe it wasn't different, but it seems a little different. That's not what I'm asking. I'm saying, what if we found out someone who was being targeted because he was guilty of something was actually completely innocent of it. It's a hypothetical question, I understand that."

"Yeah," put in Gretchin, "and a moral question, right, Bradley? And of course, you have to do the moral thing. You never had to before, but now you do. And why, just to give a couple of twirls in the spotlight of approval? And approval from whom— Bob, the Agency, us, George fucking Washington?"

"Yes, I want to do the moral thing, I'll always want to, Gretchin, whether you make fun of me or not."

"Oh God," she shot back, "you're living in a comic book. Shit, nobody's ever completely innocent or guilty. What a dummy."

"Go ahead, I don't care, I hear it from you all the time anyway, I'm used to it."

"Do you really think that what the Agency does is ever actually moral?"

He was indignant. "Of course it is."

With an exagerated roll of her eyes, "Oh my God! It isn't, Bradley, it isn't supposed to be. The whole thing, all of it, the whole shooting match, the system, the projects, all of it, isn't about being right or someone else being wrong, it's about being stronger than they are, it's about prevailing over them, pure and simple. It's not about morality, Bradley, it's about power."

"Well, I want it to be right."

"No," she insisted, "you want it to seem to be right, you want to believe it's right. . . . You know, I've never actually thought of you as a moral guy. When you were the principal you said some pretty immoral things, as I recall. You were a bully, for one thing. You bullied the kids, and you bullied us teachers."

"Yeah, well, since then you've done nothing but try to bully me."

"Sure, it's been payback, fuckhead."

"All right, so I'm paid back, why don't you stop? Good grief, I get it every single day."

But he had pushed a button and she could not be diverted. "And when we were all dismissed from the team by the Agency, you threatened to ruin Martina's school pension. And you would have ruined it, too, if she hadn't threatened you back with Stanley's KGB friends. Only a real bastard does the things you do, Bradley, and you do them all the time. You're not actually a moral person, mister, you just talk the goddamn talk. I worked with you as a teacher, and as a team member, and now I'm your wife, and I know."

"Well, I like to think of myself as moral, I try to be moral."

"You're not a moral man, Bradley, you're a moralist. You look for approval either from the system or from yourself. You think the system is moral, and you let the system run your conscience by telling you what is moral."

"I asked a good question," he sneered, "and you're just jealous."

"That's so stupid, what in God's name would I be jealous of? What a fucking dope! You know, this question of yours makes me want to ask you one. If someone attacked your house, would you defend your house or take a seat on your goddamn couch and wonder who was right and who was wrong?"

With a shrug, "If I had time to think about it, maybe I would wonder."

"Oh that's great," she moaned. "So, if somebody was trying to hurt me or even kill me, and you had time to think about it, you would actually deliberate over who was more right or more wrong, correct?"

He raised both hands. "I don't know, Gretchin. Of course I'd defend you. But that wasn't what my question was about."

Then Coldgrave said, "Bradley, why not look at it like war, which is probably how the Agency sees it. It's the larger picture. The individual doesn't count. The individual soldier is basically innocent, too. He's drafted, leaves his family, and is largely innocent. He didn't want the war, didn't vote for it, whatever, and yet he's there. You shoot him because of the bigger picture, the war. It's how it all works."

"But in war you take prisoners."

She looked into the glass, then up at him. "Only if you think you might be able to trade them."

Now he looked around the table. "Let's ask Kelly. Kelly, what would you do if you found out a target who was supposed to be guilty was actually innocent? And say you were on the job when you found it out."

Finishing a noisy slurp of her tea, she answered, "I'd joost do what I wanted at the toime. I'd probably shoot hem anyway. Who cares?"

"Know what I think, pal?" said Packard. "I think you ask yourself this question of yours way too much, and I'll bet you ask it in all kinds of ways. You're in the wrong business, I can tell you that. Me, I've probably never been right in my life. I'm sorry it's botherin' you, bub, but you're never going to be actually right in anything you do, so just get over it."

"So, you're saying what?"

The old killer reached for his coffee. "Pick a side, pick a gun, and don't look back."

Bradley looked into the wolfish eyes. "I've done the first two, I'm not sure I can do the third."

"Then I'd say get out of the business. Hell, you've already put some people down. I hope you're not foolin' yourself by thinkin' they were completely guilty. So, if you're gonna spend the rest of your life thinkin' about them, why add to the list? If that list gets much longer, hell, you'll never sleep again. You might just want to walk away from everything now, retire, go back to being a principal."

His gaze dropped to his plate. "I'll probably just stick around."

"So," said Gretchin, "you're not going to think about these things when you're out there with us on a project, are you? I'm usually riding with you, and if you hesitate, I could get killed. And that's something I'll never consider morally right."

"What, if I hesitate?"

"No, if I get killed."

Pushing his cup away. "I guess it is a little like war. I have nothing against war. . . . All right, I think I'm okay with everything. I'm fine."

"God!" she uttered, "this has been a pathetic conversation."

He shot her an angry look. "I just wanted to talk things out, that's all. You don't have to jump on everything I say, Gretchin."

"So, you've talked it out?"

"Yeah, sure."

"Bullshit."

"No, I'm fine."

"So, I can have my goddamn dessert now, in peace maybe, without you asking your stupid questions?"

"Yeah."

CHAPTER 28

Nearly a month later Maggie watched the yellow Corvette swing around the fountain and stop at the front steps. She waited until Gretchin had gotten out, then released the curtain. She did not need to see the whole drama, for she had witnessed it many times and always it seemed to be the same. The two would return from some jaunt, Bradley would drive once around the fountain, stop at the front steps for her to get out, all the while drumming his fingers on the steering wheel. He would sit and continue the drumming as she stood with her door open excoriating him for some sin of commission or omission. Finally she would slam the door, and leaving him to park the car and bring in the bags, she would march, not walk, into the house.

"I need a drink!" exclaimed Gretchin as she reached for a hanger for her coat. "That man's such a pain to travel with. God!"

"Have a good time?" queried Maggie pleasantly, as if the other had not said a thing.

A short stare, then, "Of course."

"You look like you've gotten some sun."

Gretchin ran a hand through her hair. "I love the Bahamas," she replied, "it's a wonderful place to drink and screw, but that sun's mean as hell—I'll probably get skin cancer from it."

"Well," replied Maggie, casting a glance at the dragon tattoo, "it can give you wrinkles."

"Yeah, and turn your goddamn hair white."

Casting another glance, this time at the grayed red hair, "Yours still looks impressively intact, dear, I wouldn't worry about it." But immediately she winced at using the term, for it had always been nearly reserved for Martina.

With a glance, "You never call me *dear.*"

Averting her gaze, "Yes. . . . Sorry."

"You miss her, don't you? You don't need to answer, I do too, Maggie. I can't really believe she's gone, you know."

A long sigh. "I know."

For the most part the vacations had gone well. Maggie and Packard had volunteered to keep to the Estate. While Gretchin and Bradley had gone to the Caribbean, and Connors and Bobbie Lee to Ireland, Coldgrave had gone by herself to Paris. Within thirty days, all were back at the Estate.

"I should let everyone know," said Coldgrave that evening at dinner, "that my vacation did not go undisturbed."

"He *didn't,*" said Maggie, setting a hot pie on the table and taking her seat.

Coldgrave lifted her glass. "He did. I had been there only three weeks or so—I'm not good at math—and he called." And with a dreamy look, "It was all beautiful. Countless bars and restaurants. Wonderful."

Bradley shot Packard a roll of his eyes, as if to say he doubted the 'restaurants' part.

"But Mary," said Maggie, "since you're not good at math, how are you so good at figuring ballistics and understanding the technical side of weapons?"

Setting the glass down, "Good question. I think, because weaponry is part of my DNA, whereas math, at least socially, is not. . . . Anyway, he called and interrupted my fantasy of escaping the Agency's radar."

Gretchin wrinkled her nose. "Well, he didn't bother me. Guess he doesn't love me."

"And I'll bet," said Bobbie Lee, "that jist about breaks your heart."

"So," said Bradley, reaching for one of the little plates of pie, "he's got a new project for us, Mary?"

"I'm afraid so."

On impulse, he said, "Tell us about the bars." But when Gretchin shot him a look, he modified the question. "I mean, did you have a good time?"

Coldgrave checked the ice in her glass. "Yes, I did, Bradley."

His eyes moved from the hair to the pearly skin to the asymmetrical eyes to the lipstick. "What kind of bars do they have in Paris? Do they have shows and stuff?"

"The bars I went to were of course upscale, not rustic."

"You mean, not disreputable?"

She shrugged. "Whatever. As for shows, yes, some presented shows, some had dancing, some just quiet music, usually live music. It was all very nice."

"So, did the shows have—"

As he stopped there, she offered, her right eye resting upon him, "Nudity?"

"I don't know, I suppose, yeah."

She watched as his shoulders rose, seemed to stay there, then fell. It would have been comfortable to see him as odd, to dismiss him that way. But the uncomfortable truth was that he was not odd at all but painfully typical. Finally she said, "One show had nudity, yes."

"All right, Bradley," put in Gretchin, clearly uncomfortable, "why don't you just button it, you're not doing well here."

But Coldgrave said, "These bars, and yes, some of them were nightclubs, were very nice, Bradley, definitely artistic, so to speak. But I would offer the caveat that none of them provided an atmosphere in which you would have enjoyed yourself. At least, not as to the clientele."

He frowned. "What's that mean? Were they weird?"

"Bradley," said Gretchin, increasingly annoyed, "don't be a donkey please."

"Sure," he returned. "I just wanted to know."

And he does want to know, Coldgrave mused as she looked at him sitting there with his silly grin. In fact, they all want to know more specifically what kind of place it was where Bradley would not have enjoyed himself. Yes, he was right on target with his term *weird*. She could easily satisfy their curiosity with a full description of the topless show and the clientele that had attended it. She could go on and tell them about one of the dancers, a beautiful French girl, whom she had met with backstage after the show. She could paint for them the ambience of the piano bar where they spent the rest of the evening drinking and dancing. She could even describe the sharing of the martini and comparing of lipstick marks on the glass. She could do that, yes, but to what purpose other than to further feed their curiosity and give them more tools with which to reach into her heart? No, she would not do it, she would not tell them. For very simply, her private world was too precious to her and much too necessary for her peace, to subject it to their scrutiny.

Gretchin shook her head. "It's not your business, bub. Drop it."

Then he said to Coldgrave, "Bet you paid a hundred dollars a drink."

"I wouldn't know," she replied.

"Come on, sure you do."

"I use a card, and cash if I need to. If I ever see a bill, which is rarely, I forward it, and my lawyer pays it. . . . But then, you've asked me these things before, Bradley. Surely you remember."

"Oo-o-o," said Gretchin gleefully, "that was perfect."

Undaunted, he continued, "But you look at the bills, you look them over, right? I mean, even sometimes?"

She was thoughtful for a moment. "No, I don't look them over, I just forward them."

"But what if a bill's wrong?"

"What if it is?"

"You don't even check the bill's total?"

She brought the glass to her lips. "No."

Rolling his eyes, "But is that even responsible?"

"What would it have to do with responsibility?"

He blinked. "I've noticed when you pay with cash, like for drinks, you never get change, even when the change would be ten or twenty dollars or even more. Why is that, why don't you want your change?"

"What would I do with it, Bradley, keep track of it?"

Bobbie Lee, watching as his expression changed to sheer unbelief, uttered, "Jesus, that's rich. Man, I wish I was that rich. Mary, if I had your money, I'd buy mysilf somethin' real nice every day."

They all watched as Coldgrave did not reply but merely looked into her glass, then got up and left for the kitchen. They were silent until she had returned with her fresh drink, continuing to watch as she took her seat and reached for a plate of pie. She seemed quite unaware of being on stage as she took a sip of the gin, paused to swallow it pleasurably, then took up a tiny piece of the pie and ate it.

"So," said Bradley, following as the fork slid from the red lips, "you've really never seen a complete bill?"

With the fork she separated another small piece of pie. "You know what, Bradley, I'm sure I've seen one, I must have. I'm sure I saw one in college, in the practical classes, you know, business, economics or whatever they called them. So, there you are, I'm sure I've seen, well, probably hundreds of bills, who knows?"

He said nothing further, but ran a hand over the top of his crew cut, reached for his fork, scooped up half his wedge of pie, and put it into his mouth.

"Okay," said Packard, "now that we've walked around in all this bullshit, what's the plan for the next project, who drives?" And to Bobbie Lee, "How's the leg?"

"Jist about perfict. No wheelchair on the trip, only crutches, and even walked without 'em sometimes. Got the cast cut off over there. But yeah, now I'm ready to rock and roll."

"Motorcycle?"

"Maybe. I'll sure give it a try, if necessiry."

"Ah," protested Connors, "you're, loike, stell lempin', forgat et. I'm not climbin' on no motorcycle weth you. I'm not lookin' to gat me ass burned off. Besoides, et's too fuckin' cold out, what's wrong weth yous, loike?"

"No offense," said Packard, "I just wanted to know how many bases were covered."

Then Gretchin asked, "Mary, did he say what the project involved?"

"No, he only said he would come to see us when we were all back."

CHAPTER 29

"I have to say," said Willard as he and a sidekick agent sat on the couch and munched cookies, "that the vacation seems to have agreed with everyone."

Maggie smiled. "What makes you say that, Bob?"

"Oh," he muttered, dropping half the cookie, "well, everyone just seems refreshed somehow, I don't know, but it's definitely there, the atmosphere, I mean."

"Bob," said Coldgrave, "how is Sandy? It was so nice you could bring her for—for Easter."

"She's fine, yes. But wasn't that just before Christmas?"

She put her glass down. "You're right, Bob, yes, it was Christmas."

Taking her seat beside Packard, Maggie said, "You're a very lucky man, Bob, as I'm sure you know."

He beamed. "I do."

With a chuckle, Bobbie Lee pushed herself up, stepped over to the tea cart, and pulled a beer from its ice bucket. Returning to her seat beside Connors, she took a swig, then looked over at the sidekick agent and said, "Hey, what's your name again, Bo?"

When the agent said nothing but simply stared at her, Willard replied, "Rich, his name is Rich, I just introduced him."

"Oh, that's right," she returned, getting herself more comfortable on the chair. "Well, you know what, Rich? I'd like to know what you've been lookin' at." When again he did not respond, she said, "I mean, you put your eyes on me the moment you walked in. You got a problem with me, or somethin'?"

When the agent's gaze instantly dropped Willard said, "Rich, everything all right?"

"Uh, yeah, sure," came the reply, "not a problem, sir."

"Sorry, Bobbie Lee," said Willard, "Rich kind of stares, he's just curious. Rich, tell Ms. Henry you didn't mean anything." After the agent had shaken his head in acquiescence, Willard added, "Ms. Henry is a nice lady and a valuable part of the team. She does a great job for us. . . . Everything okay, Bobbie Lee?"

With an askance look, "Sure, Bob. I jist thought ol' Rich here might be starin' at my muscles. 'Cause if he was, I can git him a couple of magazines to look at."

Willard's eyes went closed. "No, no, everything's fine, just fine, we're okay here."

"So, Bob," put in Coldgrave, "do you want to tell us about the new project?"

"Yeah," said Gretchin, "it nearly slipped your mind, didn't it, Bob?"

"Funny," he returned, "very funny. Now let's get down to business, if we can."

"Oh," she said, "you're saying we've interrupted you?"

"Just my train of thought, that's all. But I'm fine, let's go on."

"But," she persisted, "what did you mean by *if we can?*"

The agent Rich could contain himself no longer. "Why don't you just give him a chance to talk? Every time he opens his mouth, you or somebody else interrupts him."

Quickly Willard turned to him and said in a shocked whisper, "What? Why did you say that?"

Shrinking, the agent replied meekly, "Because you were being interrupted, sir. It was rude, I had to say something."

"Thanks, Rich, but please."

"So," said Bobbie Lee, "this guy doesn't know when to keep his eyes in his head or his mouth shut."

"No, no, he's fine," Willard came back quickly. "But I'll take it from here, Rich, if it's okay."

The agent looked back and forth from Bobbie Lee to Connors, his face now a bright red.

As Willard sent a pleaful look in Bobbie Lee's direction Coldgrave said, "Why not tell us about the project, Bob?"

"Darn, Mary," he blurted, "I'm trying to do that."

"Ah, come on," said Bobbie Lee, "jist because you're frustrated, Bob, you don't have to go swearing at Mary here."

Nearly choking with frustration now, he said, "Sorry, Mary, I didn't mean to be abrupt. I apologize, I do."

Coldgrave took a sip of her drink, then replied, "No harm done, Bob. Continue."

Swallowing hard and throwing a cautious glance in Bobbie Lee's direction, he said, "All right, the new project. Well, I personally am very happy to say that this one should be simple, straightforward, and require minimal firepower. Actually I think Mary, Gretchin, Bradley, and Kelly should be sufficient. This is only my suggestion, of course, and I'll leave it to Mary to make the final decision as to who should go. Anyway, you will have three targets—a brother and sister and their friend. They're living in the northeast part of Philadelphia. They're in a single house, rented, of course, and they have one car, also rented, a Honda Civic. There's not too much surveillance info on when they come and go, but again, they only have one car. They're not believed to be heavily armed, and haven't visited any of the local gun ranges. So, it should be pretty simple. Specifics from intel, with photos—only three, but color—are in here." And with a smile of satisfaction, he patted a large envelope beside him.

Bradley cleared his throat. "So, no more Florida jobs? I like to travel, but it seems we've gotten a lot of locally based projects lately."

He smiled. "Simple answer—funding. We're waiting for the new budget to be put together, but for right now we're trying to match teams with projects in their localities." And throwing Gretchin a flickering glance, "So, the Agency isn't being cheap, just frugal. Most of the projects for all the teams can be executed through car travel."

"I have another question," said Bradley, bringing his foot to his knee and looking at the ceiling. "Could I ask, Bob, what they've done."

Hesitating, "Done? You mean, work?"

A sniff. "No, I mean, what crimes."

"Sure, I was just going to say, they've been operating as explosives merchants. No one dead yet as a result of their dealings, but their connections have grown to the point where the Agency says they must go."

Pulling his shoestring loose and retying it, Bradley looked at him, then said, "But that's not a capital crime."

Willard blinked. "No, it isn't," he replied. "But the Agency has decided they have to go, that's all. They can't be arrested, if that's what you're getting at. It's imperative that they not be arrested. These people cannot be allowed to make any further connections, either inside prison or out. . . . This team was not formed to apprehend people, but to eliminate them. But of course, you know that, Bradley, so why do you ask?"

He picked at the shoe.

Gretchin, who had been watching her husband closely, spoke. "He's become sensitive about the morality of our work. Maybe you've gotten to his conscience, Pastor Bob—you know, with all your bullshit."

Willard looked at her, then at Bradley, then back at her. "Sensitive? Really? In this business?"

"Yes. He wants to make sure he's doing the right thing when he blows someone's head off."

"And you're blaming me, Gretchin?"

"Just a little."

"That's preposterous. That's absurd."

"Why is it absurd?" she returned heatedly. "You've been trying to get us to be safer, more sensitive, and even religious. Every single time you come around here you praise him and describe the rest of us as brutes or savages. You know he agrees with you, so you practically jerk him off with all your American-flag stuff. You two deserve each other. It's not absurd at all, it's perfectly logical. Congratulations, Pastor Bob," and pointing to Bradley, "here's your goddamn Frankenstein."

Mouth open, he stared at her, then at Bradley. Finally he said, "Bradley, what the heck's going on? You knew what you would be involved in when you agreed to be part of the team. Now you're questioning the Agency's wisdom?"

Bradley looked at the floor. "I don't know, I just want things to be right, that's all. I'm not questioning the Agency. This is war, I know that."

Willard closed his eyes. "No, it's not war, Bradley. Our work is actually to prevent war."

His head bobbing, "Yeah, yeah, sure, I understand that, and I'm on the same page as you, that's a fact. But I just want to have a clear conscience that I'm not killing people who don't deserve it."

As Willard's face filled with astonishment and Bradley's with confusion Coldgrave said, "Bob, this issue has been on Bradley's mind for some time now. He brought it to us as a group, and we listened to him and reasoned with him, but his views are still quite strong."

"Then why didn't you call me, Mary, and tell me about it?"

Here she lifted her drink and delicately smelled it. Then she took a sip of the cold alcohol, held it in her mouth for a moment, and swallowed it.

"This is important," he insisted, "I should have been told."

"Maggie," said Coldgrave, "thank you so much, this is perfect, not too much ice, but the ice is excellent, too."

"They said the ice had just come in," returned Maggie, obviously pleased. "And I did notice that the bags looked especially clean and the pieces of ice very clear and not stuck together."

Willard, whose eyes had gone shut again, raised his head. "Bradley and everyone," he said, fatigue in his voice, "let me just say this." And taking a deep breath, "I am the contact for this team. I speak to you on behalf of the Agency."

"Oh God!" cut in Gretchin. Then, with some melodrama, "I can smell the bullshit coming, it's almost here. Go ahead, Bob, the floor is yours."

For a long moment he did not speak. He looked first at Coldgrave, then at Bradley, then for a moment even into Gretchin's mocking eyes. Slowly he rose to his feet, motioned for Rich to get up, then handed the envelope to Coldgrave. Making no attempt to hide his frustration and disappointment, he said, "Here, Mary, it's all in there. Call me if you have any questions." He turned quickly then to leave, but stopped abruptly and said directly to

Bradley, his tone quite serious, "Oh, and, Mt. Hopkins, just kill them, okay?"

Close behind him, Rich stopped, turned, and ventured one last glance in the direction of Connors and Bobbie Lee. They were grinning at him, as if in unison. His eyes met Bobbie Lee's, and he watched as she simply raised a hand and gave him the finger.

CHAPTER 30

Philadelphia, Early March

Making a right at the corner, Bradley said, "Not many people out, that's good."

"Yeah," said Gretchin from behind him, "good for your new image."

He tightened his grip on the wheel and in singsong replied, "You're being critical."

"You know, if you joined a church, you could get hardcore points for all this change in your personality." When he didn't respond she added, "I'm going to miss the old you, Bradley. You know, the bully, the bastard, that kind of thing. Some people might prefer the new self-righteous you, but for me, at least before, you were honest about being a shithead."

He tried to ignore her, but felt his face becoming hot with embarrassment. After turning the final corner he pulled to the curb two houses from the targets' split-level. "We're going to get a storm, they say, a big one. This place is going to be under about a foot of snow in a week. Hard to believe—in March—weird."

With a gloved finger, Coldgrave touched the corner of her mouth, then put the visor up. "Anybody need to see the photos again?" she queried. When there was no response she returned them to the envelope, then pulled the .38 from her purse and swung the cylinder free. Snapping it back in place, she gave a long sigh and listened to the sweet sounds of holster snaps and gun metal as the others checked their weapons.

For a moment she closed her eyes and let her mind go back. How her heart had fluttered as she received the little wave from the dancer she had been watching, and then how heavily her heart had pounded as she made her way backstage after the show. How enthralling it had been to walk into the dressing room. The lights, the chatter, the makeup, the lipstick, the perfume, the sight and smell of it all—how she had felt she was falling into a magic, living, crystalline dream. And then her face as she got up from her dressing table, offered her hand, and said her name was Chloe. The emerald eyes, the small nose, the rubied lips, the dark hair, the snowy, doll-like skin, and the unearthly scent of the body—how authentic!

"Uh-oh," said Bradley. "One of the guys just came from around back. . . . He's getting something from the car. That Civic's a nice little car. Those things get great mileage. Not a lot of power though. I like power—lots and lots of power."

They watched as the man retrieved a laptop and a paper bag, then closed the trunk and walked toward the back of the house again.

"Mary?" said Gretchin.

Coldgrave said nothing for a moment, then, "Give me the card."

From a satchel Gretchin drew an envelope and handed it up. "Here. Who goes?"

"You and I," returned Coldgrave, drawing out the card, and then a pen from her purse.

Wincing, Gretchin said, "Just say *you and me*, would you, Mary? It's so much easier for the rest of us."

Absentmindedly, "Yes, of course, you and me." And after writing on the card, "Bradley, Kelly, get around to the back the moment you detect action."

"Right," returned Bradley, drumming on the wheel with his fingers.

But immediately Gretchin said, "Don't do that."

"Sure."

"But you know it bothers me, don't you? And that's why you did it. Everybody thinks I pick on you, but you plan your little shit stuff, don't you?"

"No."

"You're a liar. No God points there, pal."

"Stop, Gretchin, would you?" Then he said, "So, you think they're all in there, Mary?"

"They have only one car, and intel said they don't go out much. Let's take the chance."

With a shake of his head, "We don't want to miss one of them."

"But, Bradley," said Gretchin, "the one that gets away might be innocent, what about that?"

His eyes found hers in the mirror. "Shut up, would you?"

"Fuck you, asshole. Just do your job."

"I will, dear."

With a warning tone, "And don't hesitate."

"I won't."

"All right," said Coldgrave, "we're going to do this, as much as possible, in one fluid motion. Bradley, when we start shooting or go inside, drive fast to the back. Kelly, shotgun your way in through the back door."

"So, just to get it straight," he said, "even if there's no shooting, and you go inside, we go, right?"

"Correct."

From under the seat he drew out a crowbar and laid it beside him. Then he pulled the shift, accelerated, pulled them up just before the entrance to the driveway, and kept his foot on the brake as Coldgrave and Gretchin got out. He watched as they took the sidewalk that led to the front door of the house.

When they reached the slab landing Coldgrave took one look back at the SUV, while Gretchin closed her hand upon the 9mm in her jacket pocket. Then, card in hand, Coldgrave depressed the button. After a moment she pressed it again. Slowly, almost cautiously, the inner door was pulled open. A woman appeared, clearly the female target in the photos, who then unlatched the hook on the storm door and pushed it open a little.

Presenting a broad, congenial smile, Coldgrave held out the card for the woman to take and said, "Hello, I'm Mary and this is Gretchin, we're your neighbors from the next block. We're having a shower for my daughter and would like to invite you to come. You don't have to bring a gift, just yourself."

As the woman reached out and took the card Coldgrave grabbed the edge of the door and pulled it open. Instantly Gretchin drew the 9mm, shoved it forward at the woman's chest, and fired twice— *Blam! Blam!* The woman's eyes popped wide as she screamed, then fell backward to the floor, where she writhed. Even as Coldgrave pulled the .38 and stepped inside she heard the SUV roaring up the driveway and around the Civic. A second later she put the gun to the woman's forehead and fired—*Plop!*

The two women, guns aloft, moved quickly to their right and into the living room. A man, who had been watching the TV was now on his feet, his arm extended toward them, as if to push them back.

"Get out!" he yelled even as both Coldgrave and Gretchin fired. Crumpling to his knees, for he was a big man, he glared at them, then yelled, "Jimmy! Jimmy!" But they were his last words, for both guns flashed again, and he fell forward upon his face.

As shotgun blasts came from the back of the house Colgrave and Gretchin turned toward the stairs. But they stopped halfway when a horrific series of blasts rang from the kitchen and then Connors' voice called out that they had gotten him.

In the kitchen, under the table, the third target lay in a grotesque mess of flesh and blood, his whole face and one ear blown completely away. Upon the table were a plate of fried eggs, a cup of steaming coffee, and a newspaper spread open at the comics. After looking at the oozing corpse, then stepping back from the collecting pool of blood, Coldgrave said she supposed it was he.

"Just say *him,* Mary," said Gretchin. Then, "Don't get that on your shoes."

As the other took another step back Bradley queried whether they should check the rest of the house.

"I suppose," replied Coldgrave, her eye moving from the blood-sprayed wall to Connors' blank face and her smoking shotgun.

But no one else was found, and within minutes they were back in the SUV and Bradley was turning them around.

"Okay if we go home the same way?" he queried when they were on the street.

"That would be fine," replied Coldgrave, reaching for her phone. Moments later, "Hi, Bob. It's done. We're heading home. . . . No, everybody's fine. . . . No resistance, no. . . . All right, bye."

They were all silent as Bradley drove through the suburban streets, and they watched as Coldgrave snapped the Agency flip phone shut, dropped it back into her purse, then withdrew her personal smartphone.

As the screen brightened Coldgrave glanced out her window at the array of life. Then she looked at the screen and read, but only to herself, *I miss you. I love the name Mary. Paris is beautiful.* Then she pulled off a glove and typed, *I love the name Chloe. I will be coming over soon.*

Bradley, who had been trying to watch her as he drove, said, grinning, "Who's that, a boyfriend?"

Instantly and without a word, Gretchin unsnapped her seatbelt, reached up and slapped him hard on the side of his head.

"Ow!" he yelled, a hand going to his ear. Steadying the car, "You hurt me, what the heck was that for?" And when he heard no response but only the seatbelt being refastened, "You hurt me, Gretchin! My ear hurts like anything! Why'd you do that, what did I do?"

But as no answer came, he merely gritted his teeth and resolved to get his revenge later. The drive back to the Estate would not take long, unless Mary needed to stop for something to drink. Once home he would take the Vette out, alone, for a few wild sprints over the local roads, for there was nothing like feeling that kind of power and freedom.

Gretchin looked out her window at the bleak sky, which reminded her of her own pen-and-inks. It would be good to get back in the studio. There, alone, away from everyone and all their bullshit, she would relax, live, and even dream.

Connors too looked out, to where the red of a stoplight seemed nearly to drip. She was not going home, not truly, although Bobbie Lee would be there. Spring was coming, and soon the summer would allow them to walk the dogs and swim in the pool. But no, she was not truly going home. Someday, hopefully not alone, she would indeed go home, back to where the beer was dark and the grass was green.

Coldgrave, as if unperturbed by the events of the day, simply dropped the phone back into the purse, put her head back, and closed her eyes to enjoy the ride. A distinct feeling of not being alone began to come over her. The feeling, as if it had come from a glass, made her smile inside and took her mind and her heart far away to a dressing room and someone there who could enjoy a lovely dirty martini.